"CAN YOU GET IT ON THE SCREEN . . . ?"

asked Captain Benjamin Sisko. Lieutenant Commander Jadzia Dax frowned with concentration as her hands flew over the monitor.

"I'm working on it," she murmured, not really a response. The snowy static crackled and fritzed, then blinked twice and suddenly cleared.

Quite clear. Damned clear. *Damned clear—*

So close Sisko could nearly reach out and run his hand along the etched hullplates, a pure white gull-winged angel passed before them like an untarnished shipwright's model.

"That's—" Dax began, but didn't finish. Sisko parted his dry lips.

"Kirk's ship. The *Enterprise!*"

Look for STAR TREK Fiction from Pocket Books

Star Trek: The Original Series

STAR TREK
DEEP SPACE NINE®

TRIALS AND TRIBBLE-ATIONS

A novel by Diane Carey
Teleplay by Ronald D. Moore & Rene Echevarria
Story by Ira Steven Behr & Hans Beimler & Robert Hewitt Wolfe
"The Trouble with Tribbles" television episode written by David Gerrold

With an Introduction by David Gerrold

POCKET BOOKS
New York   London   Toronto   Sydney   Tokyo   Singapore

An *Original* Publication of POCKET BOOKS

POCKET BOOKS, a division of Simon & Schuster Inc.
1230 Avenue of the Americas, New York, NY 10020

A VIACOM COMPANY

This book is published by Pocket Books, a division of Simon & Schuster Inc., under exclusive license from Paramount Pictures.

ISBN: 0-671-00902-8

First Pocket Books printing December 1996

10 9 8 7 6 5 4 3 2 1

POCKET and colophon are registered trademarks of Simon & Schuster Inc.

Printed in the U.S.A.

TRIALS AND TRIBBLE-ATIONS

INTRODUCTION
Trials and Tribble-ations

by David Gerrold

I have now spent more years on this planet known as "the guy who created the tribbles" than I spent wondering what I would be when I grew up; if I had known I was going to be "the guy who created the tribbles" for the rest of my life, I might have thought twice about it.

When I wrote it, I just wanted to write one good *Star Trek* episode, just to prove I could do it. And I was deliberate about two or three things in the script. In particular, I wanted each of the ancillary characters to have something important to do, not just open hailing frequencies or fix the doubletalk generators. One of the things that I had learned in Irwin R. Blacker's screenwriting course was that "every character gets his page."

DIANE CAREY

I loved these characters; not just Kirk and Spock, but McCoy, Uhura, Scotty, and Chekov, too. I wanted each and every one of them to have at least two or three good pages. And I think that's one of the reasons why they all enjoyed the script so much; it was a chance to show a different side of their characters, a chance to have some fun.

For me, of course, the real fun was watching the actors say the lines I had written. I had been watching them for weeks, studying the way they talked; I spent hours on each scene, listening to their voices in my head, trying to match the way they spoke in the dialog I wrote.

And, of course, there was other stuff to learn, too; one day, for instance, producer Gene L. Coon pointed out to me that there were no pockets in the uniforms. "But where do they keep their money?" I asked.

"We don't use money. We use credits."

Okay. . . .

When William Shatner and Leonard Nimoy and the others finally brought the dialog to life, I was thrilled; they found things in the script, ways to say the lines, things to do with the action, that made the whole thing even funnier than I had imagined.

The only real disappointment for me came as a result of having written in a single line for myself. The part of Ensign Freeman. And Gene L. Coon had told me I could play the part; but then at the last moment, it didn't happen. I was too young-looking. Too skinny. So Shatner's stand-in got my line of dialog. *sigh*

"The Trouble with Tribbles" was first broadcast on

2

December 29, 1967. I had just graduated from college, and I invited all my former classmates over to my house to watch the episode with me. They watched it as an episode and had a terrific time. I watched it as a terrifying collection of production values that mostly worked, sort of, but not quite the way I had imagined it, and, oh, dear, why did they use that take instead of the other one?

That's the problem with being on the soundstage; later on, when it's all put together, you can't see the show; you can only see the production of it.

But my family and friends enjoyed the episode, and they congratulated me on my first professional credential, and it was otherwise a wonderful night. But I remember, quite clearly, that at one point I said, "It's only a television show. Thirty years from now, who's going to remember it?"

Duh.

The answer was, everybody is going to remember it!

But at the time, who knew? Right?

My first hint that the tribble episode had made any impact at all was when I found out it had been nominated for the Hugo Award for Best Dramatic Presentation. It was on the same ballot with "Amok Time" by Theodore Sturgeon; "The Doomsday Machine" by Norman Spinrad; "Mirror, Mirror" by Jerome Bixby; and "City on the Edge of Forever" by Harlan Ellison.

"City on the Edge of Forever" won the Hugo, as well as the Writers' Guild Award. And, yes, I was disappointed. Since then, a number of polls have been taken among *Star Trek* fans as to what is their favorite episode. In some polls, "City on the Edge of Forever" is voted the best episode of the original series; in other polls, "The Trouble with Tribbles" is voted the most popular. Either way, it's no disgrace to be in a neck-and-neck horserace with a Harlan Ellison script.

During the years that followed, I went on to other television shows; none that inspired me as much as *Star Trek,* of course, but each was fun in its own way. I developed *Land of the Lost* for Saturday-morning television; it's a show that continues today in reruns. I did scripts for *Logan's Run, Tales from the Darkside, Twilight Zone, The Real Ghostbusters, Superboy,* and *Babylon 5.*

I also wrote a few novels: *When HARLIE Was One, The Man Who Folded Himself, Moonstar Odyssey, A Matter for Men, A Day for Damnation, A Rage for Revenge, A Season for Slaughter, The Voyage of the Star Wolf, The Middle of Nowhere, Star Hunt, Under the Eye of God, A Covenant of Justice, Deathbeast, Chess with a Dragon,* and a few others. Several of these were also nominated for the Hugo and Nebula awards.

In 1994, I wrote a story about my son's adoption, "The Martian Child," and it was my first sale to *The Magazine of Fantasy & Science Fiction.* In 1995, "The Martian Child" won the Hugo, the Nebula, and the Locus Readership Poll.

So . . . yes, I have had a career outside of *Star Trek;* a rather successful one at that. But I was still being introduced as "the guy who created the tribbles."

Occasionally, someone asks me if I mind; well, yes and no. Yes, I mind that some of my later (and, I think, better) work gets overshadowed. But no, I don't mind, because the tribbles have opened a lot of doors for me; indeed, the tribbles opened the first and most important door. "The Trouble with Tribbles" was my first professional sale and gave me high-profile credentials in my chosen field of science fiction. The tribbles were my launch pad, so I've always felt a strong attachment to them.

Flash-forward twenty-nine years.

In the summer of 1996, Ira Steven Behr, Ron Moore, and René Echevarria, producers on *Star Trek: Deep Space Nine,* decided they wanted to do a special episode for *Star Trek*'s thirtieth anniversary. They told Executive Producer Rick Berman that they wanted to spend some extra money and use the digital technology perfected in *Forrest Gump* to insert the actors from *Deep Space Nine* into an episode of the original *Star Trek*. Berman agreed; so did the studio. So then they had to decide which episode of the original series to use.

There were several episodes they were considering. The tribble episode was only one of them. One day, they all went out to a local restaurant for an "executive lunch" to discuss the problems and see if they could make a decision. They kept coming back to the tribble episode as a likely candidate; they could have Arne Darvin, the Klingon spy, go back in time intending to kill Kirk, followed by the *Deep Space Nine* crew, who have to stop him before he does so.

But was Charlie Brill, the actor who had originally played Arne Darvin, available? Would he even want to do it?

While they were sitting there talking . . . who should come into the restaurant but Charlie Brill himself! And that decided that. It was a sign from God, or, at least, the Great Bird of the Galaxy. So that decision was made.

The script was written in secret. In fact, the whole project was shrouded in secrecy while the studio scrambled to make sure that they could get the necessary permissions from the original series actors. I didn't hear about the project until . . . well, never mind. There were rumors circulating on the Internet, on America Online, and on CompuServe, and I started getting E-mail and phone calls asking me for interviews and my opinion on the new show.

I ducked the first few calls, then called Executive Producer Rick Berman. I hadn't spoken to Rick in several centuries, not since the early days of *Star Trek: The Next Generation,* but it was as if hardly a day had passed. This is what's true about *Star Trek* friendships; they're timeless.

We chatted about this and that and the other thing, catching up on stuff, and finally got around to talking about the new *Deep Space Nine* episode. He told me how the episode had come to happen, how everybody was really looking forward to shooting it, and why so much of the process had to be kept secret for so long. Rick Berman is a true gentleman. He understood not only what the tribbles mean to *Star Trek,* but also the special place the original episode has in my heart. He said, "Y'know, if we're going to do a tribble episode, you should be a part of it."

So I told him how I'd always dreamed of being an *Enterprise* crew person. He laughed and thought it was a terrific idea. After making a couple of phone calls to make sure it was doable, he got back to me and told me it was all arranged. I was to report to the costume department the very next day.

I hadn't been on the Paramount lot in a long time, but it was like coming home. Coming through the main gate, you see the sky-wall overlooking the tank and the parking lot, a cluster of offices and sound-stages. It is the quintessential movie lot; a factory of imagination. And like all factories, it looks like a chaotic and senseless collection of disorganized and disjointed fragments—unless you understand the process. The more you understand, the more you realize just how efficient a factory this place really is. Every eight days, a new episode of *Deep Space Nine* comes rolling off the assembly line. You could do four years of classes at USC film school and still not have a sense of just how complex a film production really is, but that's a different discussion. When you have a team that really works, they work wonderfully.

The costume lab is a warehouse full of *Star Trek* costumes, everything imaginable, and a row of fitting and dressing rooms. The process of being measured and fitted is a lot like going to the tailor for your bar mitzvah suit. It's boring—except when it's embarrassing.

After the fitting, I went over to the soundstage where the current episode was shooting and introduced myself to the first assistant director, B. C. Cameron. (And just between you and me, she is a real treasure. *Deep Space Nine* is lucky to have such a talented and dedicated person on board.) I also glommed a copy of the script; it was my first opportunity to see what they were really up to.

To be real candid, I was prepared to hate it.

After all, how dare someone else write a tribble episode? The tribbles were mine, weren't they? Just who were these guys to be meddling with my story? Brimming with righteous indignation, I sat down to read "Trials and Tribble-ations."

Without giving anything away . . . Arne Darvin, now a hundred years later, goes back in time with the intention of killing Kirk and becoming a Klingon hero. The *Deep Space Nine* team—Sisko, Dax, Bashir, Worf, and Odo—go after him. While "The Trouble with Tribbles" occurs around them, they hunt for Darvin on the space station, in the storage compartments, in the bar, and, in particular, all over the *Enterprise,* up and down the corridors, in the rec room, in the turbo lifts, on the bridge—everywhere.

About ten pages into the script, I started smiling.

Twenty pages in, I chuckled.

Thirty pages in, I laughed out loud.

Forty pages in, I was guffawing.

Fifty pages into the script, I was rolling on the floor.

And when I finished reading, I was really really annoyed, because it was such a terrific script, I was jealous. How dare these guys write such a good script?!! This was one of the very best *Star Trek* scripts I had ever read. It was going to be a great episode, probably even a classic in its own right. Probably even a Hugo winner; and wouldn't that be ironic if, thirty years later, a tribble episode finally walked off with a rocket-shaped trophy?

But in a larger sense, the tribbles aren't mine. They are *Star Trek*'s. They are the audience's. The purpose of the original episode was to have fun; to give our heroes a change of pace and a chance to let their hair down and stop being so serious every week. In that regard, the tribbles were a gift—to the show, to the audience.

And once I had gotten past my momentary selfish considerations, I knew I should be very flattered that the gift had gone so far, that it was still giving. To have the original tribble episode brought back as an episode of *Deep Space Nine* is an acknowledgment of the popularity of the original show. For it to be remembered thirty years later, enough to be affectionately reused, is deeply touching to me. It's a very sweet validation.

To do this episode, not only would they have to insert digitally various *Deep Space Nine* characters into shots from the original tribble episode, but they would also have to rebuild and re-create large pieces of all of the original *Star Trek* sets, as well as specific tribble episode sets: corridors, the rec room, part of the bridge, the turbolifts, and the space station bar. They would have to match the lighting, the makeup, the film stock, the costumes, the props, the hairdos, and half a million other details.

The research needed to re-create the original *Star Trek* was painstaking. And the heroes of the day were Herman Zimmerman, and Mike and Denise Okuda, not to mention the rest of the crew in the art department. They studied blueprints; they studied blow-ups of individual frames of film. They had a new digital master tape made of "The Trouble with Tribbles" so they could study each shot in greater detail. (Then they could see the coffee stain on Mr. Spock's shirt.)

Then they started building, planning, preparing. Phasers and communicators and tricorders were rebuilt. A 3-D checker set and a desktop monitor. Bridge stations. Lights. Wall panels. Signs. Handles for the turbolifts. A curved corridor began taking shape on Stage 11 . . . and where are we going to find the right kind of orange mesh for the wall next to the ladder? Oops, hey? Look at this stuff over here that the construction workers are using.

Director Jonathan West, who also works as a director of photography for other *Deep Space Nine* directors, called Gerry Finnerman, the director of photography on the original *Star Trek*, to find out what kind of lighting he used (arc lights); and what kinds of filters were necessary to re-create "Finnerman lighting"? Remember all those orange and green and purple and blue lights on the walls?

This wasn't a new world that could just be invented; this was a world that had already been invented once and had to be re-created accurately. If any detail was amiss, hundreds of thousands of *Star Trek* fans would catch it immediately.

Fortunately, the team that was rebuilding the costumes, props, and sets of the original *Enterprise* were also *Star Trek* fans. In fact, I don't know anybody in the world who isn't . . . myself included.

So there I was, on the first day of shooting.

I was officially considered an "atmosphere person." I reported to the studio at eight in the morning. My twelve-year-old son, Sean, came with me to watch, as did Susie Miller, who works with me on a variety of projects. The costumers handed me my uniform; it came with a red shirt. Uh-oh. I immediately turned it around to see if there was a bull's-eye on the back. There wasn't. Whew! But I couldn't help wondering if someone wasn't trying to tell me something. . . .

As I changed into the uniform, Sean frowned and asked, "Where are the pockets?" Remembering what Gene L. Coon had told me almost thirty years earlier, I said, "We don't have pockets on the uniforms."

And Sean immediately asked, "But where do you keep your space money?" That's when I fell down on the floor laughing. The morning was off to a good start.

A little later, Sean asked, "Will we see Kirk and Spock today?" And I had to explain to him that Kirk and Spock would not be there. They didn't do *Star Trek* anymore. He was not happy about that. It was a bittersweet moment; I knew what he was feeling. To me, *Star Trek* will always be Kirk and Spock, too.

Once I had the costume on, I had a chance to look

at it, and myself, in the mirror. Too young and too skinny were no longer considerations. I was probably the oldest security guard on the ship; that was because I'd never beamed down.

Beyond that, however, I was struck by how accurate the entire outfit was. The original uniforms had been re-created exactly: everything—the boots, the flared pants, velour, the braid on the cuffs, and even the way everything was all tailored—was just like the costumes the original actors had worn thirty years earlier. And I was starting to feel a weird little tickle at the bottom of my spine.

After the costume department, we all headed over to the makeup lab, where sideburns and makeup were applied. Because the original *Enterprise* sets were lit with arc lamps, a much harsher light than is currently used for television filming, a different kind of makeup was required; the *Deep Space Nine* makeup team had gone back to the original *Star Trek* makeup as designed by Fred Philips.

Finally, I was ready for the camera, and I headed over to Stage 11, where the *Enterprise* had been re-created. There were at least a dozen other atmosphere people there, men and women, all dressed and made up in the original costumes. It was spooky to see all those *Enterprise* crew people again; they looked so much like the original crew that it was like traveling back in time thirty years. The tingle at the base of my spine became a cold chill.

The set was fully dressed now, lit, and ready for the

day's first shot. The walls were brightly lit, the doors worked, and the turbolifts were ready. B.C, the First A.D., placed the atmosphere people where she wanted us: "You go here. You two are walking from here to there. You're talking into a wall panel. Good, let's see a rehearsal; no, that won't do. You, count to two before you come around that corner. You two start from farther back. Good, that's it."

The prop man appeared out of nowhere and attached a balsawood phaser to my equipment belt, and now I was ready for a shot. My son, Sean, was thrilled; the phaser made up for not having any pockets.

And then Sisko and Dax appeared on the set, wearing twenty-third-century *Star Trek* uniforms; they looked terrific in them. Jonathan West, the director, rehearsed them for a bit; then we ran the first day's shot. It was a complex shot; Sisko and Dax are walking the length of the *Enterprise*'s curved corridor, while crew people hurry past them in both directions. Dax is amazed at how many people there were aboard "these old ships."

So was I. Today, there were twenty extras. On the original *Star Trek,* we never had more than seven. We had to do quite a few takes of that first shot while everybody learned how to work this new set, but after a while we all fell into the mood of it and the pace of the work picked up.

There were adjustments that needed to be made. After the first shot, for instance, the sound man came around and put foam pads on the bottom of the shoes of all the atmosphere people. Too loud. We sounded like a herd of mugatos. For budget reasons, the set had been built without carpeting.

Later in the day, for an even more-complex shot, also involving a camera tracking with the actors down the corridor, I was waiting behind a corner where a monitor was set up. I had to take my cue to enter by watching to see when the actors reached a certain point in the corridor; then I would come around the corner and cross behind them. Watching the shot proceed on the monitor was eerie; it was the original *Star Trek* all over again! Everything looked the same. It felt like the first new episode in twenty-eight years. And the cold chill at the bottom of my spine started creeping upward.

Steve Oster, one of the show's producers, came up to me abruptly: "David, in this next scene, Sisko has to hold the handle of the turbolift to tell it where to go. Is it all right if he lets go after he does, or does he have to hold onto it the whole time? Do you remember how the turbolifts worked?"

"Uh . . ." Thinking fast, I said, "If I remember correctly, it's all right to let go after the lift starts. But you'd better check with Mike Okuda. He's the real expert." It was a nice moment, being treated as if I knew something about *Star Trek* again.

During another break in the shooting, I had a chance to chat with Jonathan West. Jonathan works as a director of photography on *Deep Space Nine,* and he's directed three episodes on his own. He was surprised and thrilled to be asked by Rick Berman to direct "Trials and Tribble-ations."

Later, while waiting for another shot to be set up, Ron D. Moore and René Echevarria, (who wrote the teleplay, based on the story by Ira Steven Behr & Hans Beimler & Robert Hewitt Wolfe—Ed.) came by the set to visit; we had our pictures taken together and I congratulated them on doing such a good job with the script. It was filming even funnier than it read.

One of the video monitors was set up with a tape of the original "Trouble with Tribbles" episode, so the actors and the director could see what was happening in the scene they would be matching. For instance, in the rec room scene where Kirk discovers that his chicken sandwich and coffee arrive with tribbles, Sisko and Dax would be inserted digitally. They would be surreptitiously watching Kirk; so Terry Farrell and Avery Brooks had to watch the scene a few times to see what they would be reacting to.

As we stood around the monitor, one of the A.D.'s was searching backward through the tape for the scene until I asked innocently, "Why are you rewinding? The scene you're looking for takes place in the third act."

For a moment, a couple of folks looked at me surprised, and I felt embarrassed at having spoken up, until somebody realized, "He's right."

And then somebody else said, "Well, if anybody knows this show, it should be David."

By the second day of shooting, the atmosphere

people had become a real team. The assistant directors could give a set of instructions and the team would hit their marks every time. They were as professional a group of folks as I'd ever seen on a soundstage, and . . . well, it was like finally getting a chance to play with the big kids.

Everybody knew we were doing something special here; the cast, the crew, the folks in the front office, the studio executives, everybody connected with *Star Trek* knew we were re-creating a piece of classic television, and that if it worked, it would make television history. Everybody was jazzed and you could feel the excitement everywhere on the set. The cold chill was halfway up my spine now.

While Paramount Pictures does not have a studio tour the way Universal does, with earthquakes and King Kong and flash floods and trick bridges, they do have guides escorting small groups of tourists around the lot, showing them the workings of a real film studio. During breaks between shots, the atmosphere people would often wait outside the stage, and we often saw these groups wending their way between the soundstages. The tourists would look over and see us in our classic *Trek* uniforms and their eyes would go wide with surprise.

And it wasn't just the tourists, either; a lot of the people who worked on the Paramount lot, even actors from other shows, reacted with delight to see folks dressed again in the original *Star Trek* uniforms. It made me start to think . . . what if Paramount started a new *Star Trek* show, one that took place in Kirk and Spock's time? Or how about even a new set of shows about Kirk and Spock? (If you used a new, younger cast, you could start off by telling the story of how Kirk first took command of the *Enterprise*.) I still wonder if that's doable.

On the afternoon of the second day, one of the studio messengers offered me a ride on the back of his electric cart, and we passed a very large group of sight-seers. Half a dozen of them saw me and grinned; they lifted their right hands in the Vulcan salute. I laughed and saluted right back.

Knowing that Mike Okuda had expressed a wish to have one of the original tribbles appear in this new episode, I'd brought one to the set; and as I showed it off to Jonathan and some of the other folks from *Deep Space Nine,* some of them held it with a sense of awe, as if it gave them a mystical connection to the past.

A little while after that, John Dwyer came by; John was the set decorator for *Star Trek* and he had worked on the original "Trouble with Tribbles" episode. John is a tall guy, always smiling, always having a good time. He walked up and down the sets now, examining details with a big smile on his face. On the bridge set, he looked at the base of the chair at a work station, something that wouldn't even show up on screen, and grinned. He turned to Mike Okuda: "You even got the chairs right!"

Not only the chairs, even the graphics on the bridge stations and the buttons on the consoles, as well. Jim

Van Over, who had done much of that work, proudly pointed out how he'd duplicated all the separate details.

John and I swapped a few stories of our own—about all the folks we still remembered fondly. He had a terrific story about Irving Feinberg, the show's prop man, and how he once brought in a brand-new set of socket wrenches to be Scotty's tools. . . .

And then the high point of the day occurred. Bob Justman arrived.

Now, listen, in all of the histories of *Star Trek,* you hear a lot about Gene Roddenberry. And more recently, Gene L. Coon is starting to receive some of the credit he so richly deserves for the success of the original series. But it was Bob Justman who made it all work; he was on the soundstage every day, overseeing every detail of the production. He did it for all seventy-eight episodes of the original *Star Trek.* He did it for the first five years of *Star Trek: The Next Generation.* There is nobody alive who knows the nuts and bolts of *Star Trek* like Bob Justman. I've admired him since the day I first met him in the summer of 1967. Bob Justman combines a gentle manner with a no-nonsense approach to production that has set a standard for others to match.

I found him at the end of the curved corridor, watching the setup for a particularly tricky shot. He turned around and saw me and I just grabbed him and gave him a big hug. He saw me in the red security guard's uniform and started laughing. "You finally made it," he said.

I hadn't seen Bob since 1988, and it was like a joyous family reunion with a favorite relative. We stood and babbled at each other for a long time, catching up on old news, clearing up silly old business, and just sharing the joy of both of us being back on the *Enterprise*. I congratulated him on his new book (*Inside Star Trek,* written with Herb Solow), he congratulated me on my son's adoption, and I showed off pictures.

And the cold chill that had started at the bottom of my spine suddenly hit the top and my eyes started to fill up with tears of sheer joy. We were back on the *Enterprise* again and thirty years had disappeared. This was all we'd ever wanted to do: make *Star Trek*.

Indeed, this was the reason why all these folks were here today. They'd all come aboard this show because they'd all shared the same dream of making more *Star Trek;* and here we all were, remaking the original *Star Trek* one more time. Wow!

Bob walked the sets with Mike Okuda and other members of the art department, nodding thoughtfully. Abruptly he stopped, looked up, and said, "Those panels are too dark." And he pointed at the orange mesh next to the ladder. "And that doesn't quite match, either."

Mike Okuda's face fell. "You found the only two things we couldn't match exactly. The company that makes the reflective plastic went out of business ten years ago, and nobody makes the same kind of mesh anymore."

But then Bob said, "You got everything else right.

It's perfect. When you take this set down, will you send me one of those wall panels as a souvenir? It would mean a lot." And yes, it meant a lot to Mike and Denise Okuda and the rest of the art department, as well, to receive such high praise from the man who made the original *Enterprise* work.

Somewhere in there, I mentioned to Bob how carefully they'd even duplicated the "Finnerman lighting," and he said, "Nope, it's 'Justman lighting.' *Star Trek* was Gerry Finnerman's first job as a D.P., and I had a long talk with him about how I wanted the show lit, and why I wanted to use the colored gels to provide a mood for the sets. Do you know he was so nervous during the first season that he used to throw up after we'd screened the dailies?"

The stories you hear thirty years later . . .

But then it was time to get back to work. There was one more scene to shoot before the day was over. O'Brien and Bashir have accidentally been caught in the fight in the bar, and now they're in the lineup where Kirk bawls out Scotty, Chekov, and Freeman. (And, yes, while it would have been fun to insert me into that shot with O'Brien and Sisko so I could finally play the part of Freeman, it wasn't technically feasible. Besides, I was wearing a red shirt, re-member?)

When the lineup is dismissed, O'Brien and Bashir come down the corridor and around a corner to see that there are tribbles in the *Enterprise* corridor. First, Jonathan shot the dialog with O'Brien and Bashir; then he set up an over-the-shoulder shot of what

O'Brien sees. Because of the angle of the shot, the best place to stand was right behind Jonathan.

Abruptly, he turned around to me and said, "David, what do you think? Aren't there too many tribbles in this shot?"

"Well . . ." I started thinking out loud. "O'Brien and Bashir just walked out of the lineup. The lineup happens at the beginning of the third act, and we haven't seen tribbles out of control on the *Enterprise* yet, so this would be the first time we see how fast they're breeding; so, yes, there are too many tribbles in the shot."

Jonathan walked onto the set, and I followed him, and we proceeded to remove half the tribbles. "What do you think, David? Is this about right?" And as I answered him, I suddenly realized everyone was looking at me. For one brief moment, I was directing the director!

"This looks good," I said. And then, not unselfconsciously, I suggested, "You know, this is the shot where you should use me. You should have a crewman, kneeling down on the floor actually playing with one of the tribbles. Let me do that."

"You're right," he said. And that was the way the scene was set up.

When you watch the show—and if you're a serious fan, you've probably taped it—I'm the silver-haired security guard playing with the baby tribble; the same one I'd brought to fulfill Mike Okuda's wish. That tribble is now the only tribble to have appeared in both tribble episodes!

They ain't never gonna get the grin off this face!

And then the shot was in the can and the day was over. It was late and it was time for me to head home. I turned in the phaser for the last time. I took off the costume with real sadness. The adventure was winding down, but not really.

In truth, it was only beginning. *Star Trek* never ends. It only begins. As I left the lot, I felt young again because I'd had a chance to rediscover the fun and the magic and the dream. The final frontier is not space. The final frontier is the human soul. Space is where we will meet the challenge.

But until we get out there full-time, *Star Trek* is one of the places where we will imagine the challenge.

No, it's not enough. But it's a great start. Isn't it?

—David Gerrold, 1996

DAVID GERROLD is the guy who wrote "The Trouble with Tribbles" episode for the original *Star Trek* series. He's also written a whole bunch of other stuff, too.

Prologue

"*CAPTAIN!*"

"Kirk here."

"*I'm picking up a subspace distress call, priority channel. It's from* Space Station K-Seven."

"Go to warp factor six."

"*This is a red alert. Man your battle stations. All hands, man your battle stations. We have a Code-One Emergency Disaster Call. All hands, man battle stations . . .*"

"Captain's log, Stardate 4523.3. *Deep Space Station K-Seven* has issued a Priority-One call. More than an emergency, it signals near or total disaster. We can only assume the Klingons have attacked the station. We're going in armed for battle."

The bridge smelled fresh, clean, ready. The maintenance crew had just come through, at change of watch. The carpet was refreshed, the usual dusty residue and shavings of general activity were whisked away, and the interiors of all the computer access trunks had been scoured. The bridge looked brand-new, ready to handle anything.

"*Space Station K-Seven* on approach vector, sir." There was a crack of nervousness in the helmsman's voice. Understandable, at Priority-One alert.

"Ahead standard," Captain Kirk ordered automatically.

And the comforting response: "Ahead standard, aye."

Now the ship would reduce from warp six and come into the sensor globe of the Deep Space station at a manageable speed for close battle.

Battle. The one thing the ship was really built for, and the one thing they hoped never to have to use her for. But she was the first line of defense of the United Federation of Planets. Kirk felt his legs tense and the muscles in his arms tighten. His pulse began to match the throbbing of red alert through the ship.

Battle happened. Had in the past, would in the future.

As for the present, Captain James Kirk was ready and unintimidated. If Klingons had attacked *Deep Space Station K-Seven,* then he and this ship and crew were the rescue squad, the police, the firefighters, and the cleanup crew all rolled into one. The ship prepared itself because of red alert, bringing forward into automatic mode all the systems that otherwise would be manual, in case the crew were occupied or injured. His own body was the same, tense with grit and resistance, the weight of all with which he was saddled. He felt his posture, muscles, nerves shoring up to sustain him in whatever he had to do. And his mind, the same. More.

"Mr. Chekov, confirm weapons readiness," he said, just for his own comfort.

"Main phasers armed and ready, sir."

Kirk watched the distant dot of the space station growing larger on the screen. He had only wanted to hear Chekov's voice, to know that not only the weapons but the crew were armed and ready.

With alarming speed the three-pronged station swelled on the screen. Pushing to his feet, Kirk scanned the big screen with his eyes from corner to corner, top to bottom, for attacking ships.

He saw them in his mind, but gradually realized that he wasn't seeing any on the screen. None at all.

Not even any trading ships.

"But . . ." Navigations Officer Chekov squinted at the screen. "There's nothing there . . . just the station!"

Kirk peered suspiciously at the screen.

"Priority One Distress Call," he uttered, mystified, "yet it's absolutely peaceful. Lieutenant Uhura, break subspace silence." He moved around to the side of his command chair, looked at Uhura, then turned again to face the space station.

On the upper aft bridge, Communications Officer

Uhura played her graceful hands across the board. "Aye, sir. Channel's open, sir."

"Space Station K-Seven, this is Captain Kirk of the *Enterprise.* What is your emergency?"

He knew his voice was sharp, annoyed, but he didn't care. He wanted to sound severe. Space had ears.

After a moment, the hesitant response siphoned up through the emptiness.

Captain Kirk, this is Mr. Lurry, manager of K-Seven. I must apologize for the distress call—"

"Mr. Lurry," Kirk flared, "you issued a Priority One Distress Call. *State* the nature of your emergency."

"Uh . . . well . . . perhaps you'd better beam over. I'll try to explain."

"You'll *try* to explain. You'd better be prepared to do more than that. Kirk out." He climbed the three small steps to the upper deck. "Mr. Spock, I'll need your help. Mr. Chekov, maintain battle readiness. Lieutenant Uhura, see that the transporter room is standing by."

"Aye, sir. Transporter Room, stand by."

The space station's main office was a roomy base for its manager, generally used as a meeting hall, rumpus room, and, if necessary, additional guest quarters. The multipurpose room materialized around Kirk and Spock, and Kirk found himself standing in a relatively familiar transport cubicle of a somewhat older style. This station had been here a long time.

Before the buzz of transportation faded from his ears, he was out of the cubicle and crossing the red carpet toward an unclelike man with snowy hair who wore the emblematic station-orange one-piece utility suit.

"Mr. Lurry, if there was no emergency, why did you issue a Priority-One Distress Call?"

From the middle of the room, another man, this one a buttoned-down priestly fellow with dark hair, a gunmetal-gray suit, and a stony face announced, "That was my order, Captain."

Mr. Lurry looked instantly nervous, and motioned to the dark suit. "Captain Kirk, this is Nils Barris. He's out from Earth to take charge of the development project for Sherman's Planet."

"And that gives you the authority to put an entire quadrant on defense alert?"

"Mr. Barris is the Federation Undersecretary in Charge of Agricultural Affairs in this quadrant."

"And that gives him the authority," Spock said quietly.

It didn't, really. Kirk knew that Spock was only trying to deflate the moment before his captain embarrassed them both. Barris had authority to summon help in an emergency, but there wasn't one here. He had the authority to put the sector on alert, but not emergency defensive alert with full battle-ready status. Somehow Barris might have the authority to do parts of this, but blend the parts and things just didn't add up anymore.

Aware of how things looked to him and how they'd look on paper later, Kirk accepted Spock's deference for the moment.

Barris gestured to his right to a clean-cut young man with black hair and unfriendly eyes. "This is my assistant, Arne Darvin."

Kirk tipped his head, accepting the trouble of plain courtesy. "And this is my first officer, Mr. Spock," he said, as if parrying, and with his expression he dismissed this and demanded that Barris get back to the point.

"And now, Captain," Barris said loftily, "I want all available security guards. I want them posted around the storage compartments."

Kirk leered at him. "Storage compartments? Storage compartments?"

"The storage compartments containing the quadrotriticale."

"The what, the what? What's . . . *quadro* . . . *tritic*—"

Mr. Lurry handed him a vial of something, which Kirk spilled into his palm.

"Wheat. So what?"

"Quadrotriticale is not wheat, Captain. Of course, I wouldn't expect you or Mr. Spock to know about such things, but quadrotriticale is a rather—"

"Quadrotriticale," Spock interrupted, the Gothic baritone of his voice taking over the room, "is a high-yield grain, a four-lobed hybrid of wheat and rye. A perennial also, if I'm not mistaken. Its root grain, triticale, can trace its ancestry all the way back to twentieth-century Canada, where it—"

Kirk turned his head, partly to mask his delight. "Uh, Mr. Spock . . . you've made your point."

Lurry was still trying to keep his station from being a point of embarrassment in a Starfleet report. He filled in, "Quadrotriticale is the only Earth grain that will grow on Sherman's Planet. We have several tons of it here on the station, and it's very important that the grain get to Sherman's Planet safely. Mr. Barris thinks that Klingon agents may try to sabotage it."

With his assumptions confirmed that he and his ship had been rattled for no good reason, Kirk plowed past the station manager, advanced on the tall Federation bureaucrat and drilled a glare up at him. "You ordered a Priority-One Distress Call for a couple of tons of wheat?" he bellowed.

"Quadrotriticale!" Darvin insisted from the side.

Kirk speared the assistant with a glower, but didn't reward him with a comment.

Barris was unflapped, but attempted, "Of course, Captain, I realize that we—"

"Mr. Barris, you summoned the *Enterprise* without an emergency." Kirk swung away and back to Spock's side. "You'll take full responsibility for it."

"What do you mean?"

"Misuse of the Priority-One Channel," Spock said, "is a Federation offense."

Barris flared—what little a gravestone could flare. "I did not misuse the Priority-One Channel. I want that grain protected!"

"Captain," Lurry attempted, "couldn't you at least post a couple of guards? We do have a large number of ships passing through."

"It would seem a logical precaution, Captain," Spock mentioned quietly. "The Sherman's Planet affair is of extreme importance to the Federation."

Kirk glowered at Barris, shrugged to Spock, got a Spock-shrug back—eyebrows only—and got out the communicator. *Damn it.*

"Kirk to *Enterprise*."

"Enterprise *here*."

"Secure from general quarters. And beam down two—and *only* two—security guards and have them report to Mr. Lurry. Authorize shore leave for all off-duty personnel."

"*Yes, Captain.*"

Coming up on his toes, Barris knotted his fists. "Captain Kirk, how dare you authorize a mere two men for a project of this importance! Starfleet Command will hear about this—"

Kirk swung a hand toward the man and turned away. "I have never questioned the orders or the intelligence of any representative of the Federation."

At the last moment, he turned back.

"Until now," he added.

CHAPTER
1

"Have you ever met Temporal Investigators before?"

"I'm three hundred years old. The older a Trill gets, the more interested Temporal Investigators are in us. They think we're keeping extra years in our pockets or something."

Jadzia Dax smiled and shrugged at the same time. She glanced at her side, where Kira Nerys lengthened her stride a little to keep up with Dax.

They entered the turbolift and the soft lights caught Kira's short red hair and a mischievous flash in her eyes. "When we get to Ops, let's pretend to be working and that we forgot they were coming at all."

"This is an interesting side of you," Dax accused.

Kira shrugged. "I don't like desk jockeys."

"Are these two on the station yet?" Dax asked.

"They docked ten minutes ago."

"Then they'll be up any minute."

"Right."

"Now, you behave. Benjamin could be in deep trouble over this last incident with the *Defiant*. If these investigators get irritated, they could take it out on him."

When the lift opened, Dax went immediately to her station at the science consoles of the big space station's technical heart.

She felt comfortable here, with a specific job to do—science. She was content to leave command of the station and its defensive starship to Ben Sisko and Kira Nerys. They were both fighters. Dax, in her long, long life, had been a fighter before, but never in this persona of a tall young woman, a scholar and scientist. There was enough of Jadzia left in Jadzia Dax to let go of the previous Dax hosts. She was herself now, no longer the wizened trickster Curzon, or any of those who came before.

Still, she had been in the bodies of men for a very long time, and she remembered those pugnacious drives.

She liked who she was and where she was living and working at this moment. She was glad to be science officer and not first officer. With a glance at Kira, she noted the difference. Kira was forever caught an arm's length from each decision, having always to pause and anticipate what Ben Sisko would do in a situation, or call him up here to do it. Kira had boldly done many things in her tenure on DS9, but second-in-command could be a touchy position and Dax did not covet it.

The lift hummed behind them and she turned to look.

Dax suddenly wished she hadn't been the voice of reason. Inside the lift were two of the most straight-laced, buttoned-up, clench-keistered stiffs she'd ever seen. They even looked alike. One carried a simple briefcase, making Dax hope there was a rubber snake inside. That might at least save the day.

The two men came out of the lift and the Ops air chilled by two degrees.

Steeling herself visibly, Kira went to meet them.

"Welcome to Deep Space Nine. I'm Major Kira Nerys."

"I'm Dulmur," one of the men said, as Dax pushed out of her seat and came to join them.

"Lucsly, Department of Temporal Investigations," the other said flatly.

Dax tucked her chin and gave them a teasing look. "I guess you guys from Temporal Investigations are *always* on time."

Lucsly stared at her briefly, then looked at his partner. "Joke?"

"Yeah," Dulmur confirmed. He looked at Kira. "Where's the captain?"

Kira made an audible groan inside her throat, then turned it into "He's in his office."

Lucsly frowned. "We were told he would meet us here. This recent episode with the *Defiant* has made us very worried. Tampering with time should be left to experts, not taken into the hands of . . . non-professionals."

"Non," Kira broiled, "professionals?"

"Well," Dulmur began, but Dax stepped between them.

"The captain has a very large station to run," Dax said, "as well as a powerful fighting ship that always needs attention. People coming and going any hour of any day—Klingons, Bajorans, Terrans, Cardassians, bureaucrats . . . he's a busy man." She took Dulmur's arm and turned him once again toward the lift. "But he's expecting you. He's always willing to cooperate with those in the administrative arena."

"Are you sure you don't want anything?"

Ben Sisko heard the deep rumble of his own voice, and though he was used to the sound, he also knew there was a threatening tenor in it, give or take the situation. He didn't mean to be irritated, but these two paperwonks were already on his nerves. He had offered them a drink or coffee or anything they wanted, but in true bureaucratic convention they would accept nothing. They seemed unwilling to actually *be* all the way here. They weren't even entirely sitting on the furniture, but only committing to half a butt at any given moment.

"Just the truth, Captain," Dulmur said as he studied Sisko's personal effects while Lucsly took padds and other equipment out of their briefcase.

Sisko pulled a steaming mug from the replicator

slot and turned. "You'll get it. Where do you want to start?"

"The beginning," Dulmur said drably.

"If there is such a thing," Lucsly added.

Sisko started to grin, but then realized this guy wasn't being funny.

"Captain, why did you take the *Defiant* back in time?"

Almost launching into a diatribe about how he hadn't *taken* the ship anywhere, Sisko realized he wasn't being interviewed—he was being interrogated. They'd read the logs and they damned well knew the answers to questions like that. They were implying by their line of questioning that his logs had been if not deceptive, then incomplete.

Wouldn't work. He felt too good about that mission. Things had gone wrong, and with a midair twist, he'd made them come out right. No desk-bound statuary could make him feel bad about that.

"It was an accident," he said simply.

Lucsly crossed something off on his padd. "So you're not contending that this was a Predestination Paradox?"

Dulmur added, for any idiot present, "A time loop—that you were *meant* to go back into the past?"

Unwilling to open that particular can of scorpions, Sisko said, "Uh . . . no."

"Good," Dulmur said. "We hate those. So . . . what happened?"

Drawing a breath, Sisko offered, "This may take some time."

"Is that a joke?" asked Dulmur.

Sisko was chopped in the throat by the two men's dry stares. "No," he responded, equally dry.

"Good," said Lucsly.

"We hate those, too," added Dulmur.

"Two weeks ago," Sisko began, "the Cardassian government contacted me and said they wanted to return an Orb to the Bajorans—"

"Orb?" Dulmur interrupted.

Hurt, Lucsly looked at him. "You didn't read my report?"

Dulmur seemed ashamed, and there was a subtle communication that this would be brought up again later.

For time guys, these two sure had a lot of time on their hands, Sisko realized.

Lucsly relented. "The Orbs are devices of alien origin that are considered to be sacred objects by the Bajoran people." Sisko continued. "Each has a unique property. Like the Orb of Prophecy, or the Orb of Wisdom. The one we received was the Orb of Time, although we didn't know it at first."

Sisko gazed out the office viewport at the nearby planet of Bajor, which *Deep Space Nine* perpetually guarded by proximity alone. Sometimes the people of Bajor were glad the station was here. Sometimes they weren't. The station was Cardassian, and though now run by the Federation and administered by Starfleet, still the clawed ornament in the Bajoran system presented a hive of bad memories. In its throes after Cardassian occupation, Bajor wanted to stretch its wings, but kept bumping them on *Deep Space Nine*'s vaulting pylons.

"When the *Defiant* arrived at Cardassia Prime, we weren't sure if we were dealing with a genuine Orb or one of the many fakes that have cropped up through the years. So we were going to bring it back to Bajor for authentication. In the meantime, I had secured it in one of the crew quarters and we prepared to leave. We used an antigrav palette to move it, and I placed two Bajoran deputies to stand over it, so the Bajorans could have their own witnesses that we hadn't tampered with the device in any way. Major Kira, whom you met, is also Bajoran. She and my chief of security, Odo, escorted the Orb and its two deputies to an isolated quarters aboard the *Defiant*. Everything seemed fine. But at the last minute before leaving Cardassia, we also took on a passenger, a Terran commodities trader who had been caught on Cardassia when the Klingons invaded. We didn't know it, but this passenger was not what he appeared to be."

"Humans! I never thought I'd see a normal face again!"

Not a particularly pleasant voice, despite the convivial words. In fact, the old man's voice was strained and scratchy.

At least so it sounded to Lieutenant Commander Worf. To his Klingon ears, many things sounded grating which to others were nothing. Perhaps he paid too much attention.

Such was the fallout of working in the field of security. He had drawn the duty of taking charge of this Federation national from Cardassian custody and transferring him to *Deep Space Nine.* The first thing the old man had asked for was "real food."

Now they came into the mess hall of the battleship *Defiant,* a compact muscle of a ship commandeered by Captain Sisko to offset the frustration of immobility on the big space station. The ship had turned out to be an advantage and a powerful presence in the sector, but at the moment Worf was wishing there were some convenient treaty between Cardassia and the Federation that would allow him to refuse transport of civilian passengers. Then this tattered old man would be riding on some merchant barge.

He certainly appeared to belong on one.

The old man toddled straight to a table where Dr. Julian Bashir and Engineer Miles O'Brien sat.

Worf followed, and mentioned, "This is Mr. Waddle."

"Barry. Call me Barry," the old man said, pumping O'Brien's hand.

"We are taking him back to the Federation," Worf explained, by way of claiming he wasn't responsible for him. "He was trapped on Cardassia when the Klingons attacked."

"I'm a trader," Waddle claimed. "Dealing in gem-stones, kivas and trillium, mostly." He pointed at the replicator. "May I?"

"Help yourself," O'Brien said.

Like Rip Van Winkle awakening, Waddle approached the replicator. "Raktajino," he requested, a little more clearly than necessary.

A few moments later, the replicator produced a mug full of hot liquid. The old man removed it and drew a long breath over the steam.

"Mmmm . . . do you know what Cardassians drink in the morning? Fish juice. Hot fish juice. After six months, I was *hoping* the Klingons would invade. At least they know how to make coffee! Even if they are foul-smelling barbarians." He took a sip, then realized what he'd said and glanced at Worf. "Sorry."

With a gleam of satisfaction in his eye, the old man shuffled off to another table to sit by himself.

"Don't take it personally, Worf," O'Brien soothed.

The doctor also offered sympathy. "I rather like the way you smell."

O'Brien nodded. "Kind of a peaty, earthy aroma."

The doctor held up a descriptive hand. "With just a touch of lilac."

Worf sensed he was being teased, but without comment or farewell, he turned and headed for the exit. As he left, he heard the last shards of the conversation.

"Always makes me remember an English garden when I'm around Mr. Worf. Just like the lovely gardens around Cambridge while I was in college. And I'm sure it reminds you of the fields of Ireland, doesn't it, Miles?"

"Ireland in spring, Julian, near me old granny's bungalow. Ah, yes."

* * *

So happy to be Bajoran. Such a long time since he'd felt this way. The occupation by Cardassia had shamed him in childhood, stripped him of family and home, made fear and inadequacy a daily meal.

No longer. Today he was the guard of a sacred Orb, resting just steps away in its protective tabernacle. He would be one of the two men who would carry the Orb back onto Bajoran soil. People would want to touch him, shake his hand, interview him, ask him how he felt.

His chest swelled as he gazed at the Orb and remained at attention as if it were gazing back.

There were those who said this Orb was a fake. Why else would the Cardassians give it back?

He didn't believe that. The Cardassians had been systematically shedding everything Bajoran, giving back all kinds of people and things they'd confiscated as if now those people and things were dirty. Fine.

He was anxious for Nevis to return from the mess hall so they could talk together about how proud they were. They'd been a security team for nearly a year now and were almost family.

He sighed with heavy satisfaction. His job from now on was very easy. This was a Starfleet ship, entirely secure. No Cardassians breathing over his shoulder anymore. No Klingons salivating with suspicious desire over the power of this alien device. No one around who even knew how to read the ancient texts and use the Orb.

The planet of Bajor had been left poor and struggling after the occupation and had little to call its own, nearly nothing anyone else wanted, other than strategic location. But it had ended up, through some glitch of happenstance, to be the custodian of the Orbs. Not the origin, but at least the residence.

The Orbs had become synonymous with Bajoran identity, because it was the only identity other planets would notice. Perhaps even respect, even fear. They were mystical and magical, religious and sacred, and he was proud to be standing here in the virtual presence of a reposing god.

And that was the last thought occupying his mind when the sensation of crackling energy surged through his body, shattering every nerve and vein in his body for a split second.

He saw his own arms shoot out before him in pure physical reaction and sensed for a fleeting instant a jarring pain in the middle of his back.

His last glance as vision closed like curtains from either side was the Orb, resting in the tabernacle, and the faint image of his own falling body reflected in the device's alien skin.

CHAPTER
2

"WE TRAVELED UNDER cloak, since we had to get all the way through Cardassian space without being detected by the Klingons. We were halfway home, and I was just starting to breathe easy."

Ben Sisko relaxed in his command chair for the first time since the *Defiant* left Cardassia Prime.

"But you've got to. If you say it, he'll believe it."

Beside the helm, Chief O'Brien cajoled Jadzia Dax, but she wasn't buying into the latest plot.

"Trust me," O'Brien went on. "The next time you see him, just sniff the air and say, 'Is that lilac?'"

Dax offered her elegant smile, but said, "I have my own ways of torturing Worf. Find somebody else."

O'Brien turned his eyes to Sisko, but the captain quickly said, "Don't look at me."

Resigned, O'Brien sighed and retreated to the upper deck.

Sisko was almost instantly sorry he hadn't wanted to play. Certainly he wanted something to do on this long voyage. Cardassia Prime wasn't exactly next door. He wanted to put his hands on the helm and drive, but that was Dax's job.

He wanted to fuss with the engineering, but O'Brien was constantly doing that. He even thought about health and well-being, but Dr. Bashir was right over there, gazing with that boyish wonderment at the beauty of space on the forward screen.

Oh, well . . . what was a captain to actually *do?* If the ship was in good shape, the crew was trained and doing their jobs without prompt, the mission was going smoothly, there just wasn't much to occupy command staff. He almost started wishing some little thing would go—

The red alert klaxon whined to life automatically and the bridge lights changed to accommodate their eyes, and a thousand unseen changes instantly came into play. The ship was going into "just in case" mode.

In case of what, this time?

O'Brien's voice rang out, "I'm picking up a massive surge of chronoton radiation around—"

Suddenly the bridge seemed to twist in upon itself. For a second, Sisko saw multiple images of everything around him. Then the second was over, and everything seemed normal. Or perhaps not.

"What happened?" Sisko croaked.

As if feeling the need to respond to his useless request with a useless vocalization, Dax said, "I don't know, but we've dropped out of warp."

Sisko was about to drawl, "No kidding," when O'Brien twisted toward him and said, "Sensors are coming back on line."

"Something's very wrong, Benjamin," Dax said. "According to the navigational computer, we're over two hundred light years from our last position—"

"We're decloaking!" O'Brien interrupted.

Dax frowned at her console. "Someone's activated the transporter!"

"Deactivate it and get us back under cloak," Sisko said quickly.

She worked, but didn't appear satisfied.

O'Brien's voice had a rough croak. "I'm picking up a ship—dead ahead."

Sisko turned halfway around and looked up at the dark screen. "Can you identify it?"

He peered at the flickering, struggling viewscreen. No picture yet.

Dax pressed and plucked at her controls. "Not yet, but it's close . . . very close."

Sisko clenched a fist and said, "Chief, I need that screen!"

"I think I've got it," O'Brien murmured—not really a response.

The snowy static crackled and fritzed, then blinked twice and suddenly cleared.

Quite clear. Damned clear. *Damned clear*—

So close Sisko could nearly reach out and run his

hand along the etched hullplates, a pure white gull-winged angel passed before them like an untarnished shipwright's model. Sisko recognized the configuration as each section passed—Starfleet line-drawing shapes of the dishlike primary hull, the cigar-shaped engineering hull with its gold deflector disk, the two sizzling white antimatter nacelles lancing out in back. Yes, this was Starfleet configuration, but a form that had been corrupted over the years by more and more technology and less and less esthetics.

But still . . .

"That's—" Dax began, but didn't finish.

Sisko parted his dry lips. "The *Enterprise!*"

CHAPTER
3

"NEVIS, I NEVER saw anybody eat that much. You must be one of those people who gets thrown out of all-you-can-eat restaurants. How can you stay so thin?"

"Energy. Lots of nervous energy. Lots of nerves. You should eat more too, Major, since you're eating for two."

"Oh, I eat," Kira said in a complaining way. "I don't know who's in charge anymore—me or this baby."

"You must be very happy," the Bajoran deputy said as the two strode down the corridor from the turbolift toward the Orb quarters.

"I am," she said. "But this isn't my baby."

The young man looked at her and blinked. "I beg your pardon?"

She smiled. She loved that look on people's faces, and let the instant linger. "I'm doing a favor for a couple of friends. Good friends."

"Obviously . . . hmmmm . . . uh . . . hmmm."
Poor Nevis turned about four colors, then fixed his eyes on the door panel of the Orb quarters as if wishing he could run the last few steps.

Just as Kira raised her hand to buzz the door chime, the deck beneath her pitched sideways and cast her against Nevis, and Nevis into the corridor bulkhead. She managed to roll against the young deputy and end up with one shoulder pressed into the wall, but she stayed on her feet.

"What happened?" Nevis choked. "What was that?"

"I don't know!" She struggled to get her balance, then raised one hand to tap her comm badge, but never made contact, distracted by Nevis's sudden rush away from her.

Nevis was already plunging into the Orb quarters, perhaps acting on fear, perhaps instinct. From inside, he gasped, "Arlan!"

By the time Kira got inside, Nevis was crouching beside the collapsed body of the other Bajoran deputy.

She scanned the room quickly—Orb, tabernacle, no signs of a struggle . . . no signs of any change, except Arlan lying on the deck.

"Is he dead?" she asked clinically.

"He's been stunned!" Nevis bolted as if he'd been running.

"Could he have been thrown down by that jolt? Hit his head?"

"I don't see any bumps on his head . . . someone did this to him!" Nevis looked up at her desperately. "Someone must've come in here!"

"Well, the Orb hasn't been disturbed," she told him, "at least, not apparently." She tapped her comm badge. "Kira to Dr. Bashir. Medical emergency, the Orb quarters."

"On my way, Major."

"Thank you. Kira to Odo."

"Odo here."

"We may have a break-in and assault for you to investigate, Odo, in the Orb quarters. And you thought you'd be bored this voyage."

"Being bored would be a privilege lately, Major. I'll be right there."

"Isn't there something we can do?" Nevis demanded.

Without taking any steps or touching anything, Kira looked at the outer shell of the Orb's tabernacle. No overt signs of breakage. Still . . .

"Whatever happened," she said, "I'm sure they're working on it. They'll contact me as soon as they know something. Let's just look around first."

A thousand questions. There were dozens of possibilities.

Had they gone back in time? Had someone else come forward? Was that ship a duplicate? A replica? A joke? An illusion? Was it being projected into their sensors? Were they unconscious? Were they dreaming? Was this mind control?

Resisting the silly urge to demand a report that nobody had yet, Sisko held his breath and listened as O'Brien tapped frantically on his console. Star alignments, planets, moons, charted anomalies—they could measure down to the second.

After a few seconds, he looked up at the engineer. O'Brien's face was now turned once again to the glowing ship on the forward screen. The answer was in his stunned eyes.

"We've gone back in time!"

So much for a dream.

The answer was only usher to another thousand questions. Which part of space were they now occupying? Was the cloak secured—could they be seen? Was O'Brien right in his calculations, or had the old *Enterprise* come forward in time instead?

Before them in majesty of legend, the classic vessel hung before them, its pearly hullplates showing them how much things had changed. Now—in their own time—the majority of Starfleet vessels were no longer proclamation-white. The *Defiant* herself was workhorse-gray, pretty much the color of the metal she was made of.

Before them was a driven-snow prize, with a gold deflector dish, black lettering, and white nacelles with crackling red antimatter activity in the front, like two lit cigarettes from an old detective movie. Her softly blinking running lights were unmuted Christmas red and green, her forward and aft lights bright white. She had no intention of hiding in the darkness, as *Defiant* was doing at the moment.

Sisko quietly asked, "Verify cloak."

Strange—he had nearly whispered, as if that starship out there were close enough to hear.

It nearly was. His hand twitched to reach out, run a finger along those shining plates. He still felt he could do that. More, he *wanted* to.

"Cloak is still operational," O'Brien murmured, his voice also low, subdued. "I'll shore it up some."

"Dax . . ."

"Yes?"

"Uh . . ."

The *Defiant*'s bridge sounds surged forward into the cup of anticipatory silence. Sisko could hear his own heart beating.

Dax finally had enough and broke away from staring at the beautiful classic ship to turn. "Sir?"

Sisko kept looking at the ship. "I . . . can't think of anything to say," he admitted. "There's got to be something, doesn't there?"

She smiled, cracking the tension. "There's quite a lot."

He cleared his throat. "All right, let's get on the questions—what happened, how did it happen, how do we protect ourselves, and how do we get out of this? Consider the mission delegated. Where's the major? Find her and fill her in—make sure she's alone when you tell her."

* * *

Sisko leaned back in his office chair and gazed at the two time bureaucrats as if gazing down at them from twenty feet in the air.

"Be specific, Captain," Dulmur asked, because Sisko had deliberately not said enough and was forcing him to ask. "Which *Enterprise?* There've been five."

"Six," Lucsly said with an air of superiority.

"This was the first *Enterprise*. Constitution-class," Sisko noted.

He stopped short of adding "The original, the prototype, the legend, the exemplar."

Dulmur and Lucsly seemed to get the significance without prod. They stared at each other in confirmation of dark and sinister anticipations.

"His ship!" Dulmur croaked.

"Kirk," Lucsly filled in. "James T. Kirk."

Sisko smiled.

Admiral Nelson. Francis Drake. Captain Cook. Leif Ericson. Seledon of Vulcan. Nadee of Antares. James T. Kirk.

"The one and only," he fed in proudly.

Lucsly shook his head disapprovingly. "Seventeen separate temporal violations. The biggest file on record."

"The man was a menace," Dulmur added.

Avoiding a smile this time, Sisko felt his eyes gleam with satisfaction. They didn't like James Kirk! He felt eminently fulfilled. Bureaucrats didn't like Kirk, so Sisko suddenly liked him even better. Guys who never did anything looking down their noses at guys who did all kinds of things. He felt good, because he suddenly knew where he fit into this puzzle.

"What was the date of your arrival?" Dulmur went on.

Flashing back momentarily on that first minute with O'Brien's shocked face rattling off the details, Sisko reported, "Stardate 4523.7."

The two deskies paused, and he could tell they were both making quick mental calculations, eyeing each other to make sure neither referred to a padd for help.

Dulmur murmured, "A hundred and five years . . . one month, and twelve days ago—"

"A Friday," Lucsly pounced.

Dulmur shook his head and turned back to Sisko. "Did the *Enterprise* detect your presence?"

"Luckily our cloak was still operational," Sisko said by way of avoiding details.

"What was the *Enterprise* doing?"

"She was orbiting one of the old Deep Space stations—K-Seven, near the Klingon border. Security reported that just before we went back in time someone stunned the deputy who was guarding the Orb and broke into the cabin. Sensor logs showed that someone had beamed off the ship moments after we arrived. It didn't take long for us to realize who was behind it all."

In the now-empty mess hall, Sisko glared down at a face he'd never seen, the only person on board the *Defiant* whom he'd never met—the rescued trader

Barry Waddle. But this was only a representation on a screen, a file image for transport clearance. The man himself was gone. Gone completely. No longer on board. Damn it. Skunked by an afterthought.

"His real name is Arne Darvin," Worf explained with some obviously personal irritation. "He is a Klingon altered to look human."

Dax shifted her lanky body and drawled, "His surgeon does nice work."

Beside her, Security Chief Odo's plasticlike mask of a face showed no emotion other than a certain glow of interest in his eyes. "We're assuming he came aboard the *Defiant* for the express purpose of gaining access to the Orb."

Sisko considered all this and came to the conclusion that, if Odo was correct, Darvin's presence on Cardassia had been a willing one. Not a nice conclusion. Were the Cardassians involved in this? Or was this some kind of personal plot on Darvin's part? Did the Cardassians know he was a Klingon in disguise? Surely they'd done a bioscan in so many months . . . how deeply did this entwine, and how could it be unraveled from eighty years in the past?

Darvin wasn't on board anymore. That meant he was somewhere else and they had to get him back or endanger the future.

Sensing he was going off on the wrong tangent, Sisko decided to try a different angle of analysis. "Any idea why he brought us back to this point in time?"

"We have a theory."

Worf worked the computer console briefly, calling

up a picture of a young man with somewhat angular, pinched features and a decidedly studious look. "This is Darvin as he appeared during this time period. He is presently aboard Space Station K-Seven, posing as a Federation official."

Julian Bashir leaned in from Sisko's side. "You're saying he's a spy?"

Odo nodded. "The younger Darvin's mission was to derail Federation colonization efforts by poisoning a shipment of grain being stored aboard the station."

When Kira spoke up—asking, "Will he succeed?"—Sisko realized that his entire command staff was down here in the mess hall and entertained a fleeting thought that somebody should actually be running the ship. True, they were hanging out here adrift, cloaked, but if the cloaking device blipped, somebody would have to make a decision awfully fast. The demands of the big picture were suffusing the moment-to-moment functions of the ship. Sometimes he had trouble reconciling the two. Command of a ship was a lot different from command of a station, where he could ignore some things for certain periods. Usually a mission on the *Defiant* was specific, even if action was involved. He could concentrate on the action.

Not this time. He didn't care for this dividing-the-mind demand of captaincy. He'd found over these latest years there were two men in him—an administrator and a soldier—and they didn't like doing each other's work.

"No, he won't succeed," Odo was telling Kira.

"Eighteen hours from now, James Kirk will expose him and he'll be arrested."

"That arrest will end Darvin's career," Worf filled in. "To punish his failure, the Klingon intelligence will turn its back on him. He will become an embittered outcast."

Odo nodded and shared the explanation. "From what we've been able to piece together, he spent the next hundred years eking out a meager living as a human merchant. Then, in a final indignity, he was trapped in Cardassian space by the Klingon invasion."

Slowly they put things together and into perspective with all the nasty repercussions. They knew about time travel. Minor changes could have major repercussions one hundred years from now. And if Darvin had come back in time to make a change, chances were it wouldn't be just a small change. Few people would take that risk once the decision had been made. They—he—would make good and sure things changed. There would be no mere flap of a butterfly's wings this time.

"Trapped in Cardassian space," Sisko repeated thoughtfully, "until he hears of an Orb capable of taking him back in time . . . and letting him change the past."

"So what's he planning to do?" asked Bashir. "Contact his younger self and warn him about Kirk?"

"He could be planning to kill Kirk," Dax offered.

"Or destroy the *Enterprise*," Odo suggested, "or even the space station."

Sisko frowned at the idea of such carnage, but understood in a cold-hearted way that to Darvin most of these people were pretty much already dead anyway. He was only still around because he was Klingon and had a longer life span. But the Klingons hadn't wanted him around. That meant everybody he'd associated with for the past one hundred years was gone anyway. What did Darvin care if they went a little earlier?

"The bottom line," he finally said, "is we have to find Darvin and stop him before he changes history."

"Assuming we do that," O'Brien asked, "how do we get home?"

Dax offered one of her droll shrugs. "The Orb brought us here. Hopefully it can take us back."

Kira tucked her chin. "Problem is, we don't know how it works."

"How did Darvin figure it out?" Bashir asked.

Odo handed over the twenty-fourth-century equivalent of a telltale matchbook—a padd with information scrolled upon it. Bajoran etchings. Old ones.

Looking as aggravated as a teenager being told she wouldn't yet be allowed to graduate, Kira took the padd without waiting for Sisko to assign her the task. "I guess I'd better start brushing up on my ancient Bajoran."

She moved off, studying the padd's screen.

Sympathizing with the nitpicky task she was taking on, Sisko turned to the others. "Do we know where Darvin beamed to?"

"No," Worf said. Clearly he hadn't wanted to admit

this. "He wiped the transporter log when he beamed out. He also wiped all the logs regarding this incident, so we won't know what is coming from hour to hour."

"He could be on the *Enterprise* or on the station," O'Brien considered.

Knowing perfectly well that the risk had suddenly doubled, Sisko said, "We'll have to search both without arousing suspicion or altering the timeline ourselves. The last thing I want is a visit from Temporal Investigations when we get home."

A devilish smile tugged at Dax's lovely lips, and Sisko could tell she was enjoying some aspect of this.

"I guess we'll have to find a way to blend in," she said.

57

CHAPTER
4

A HAND EMERGING from a gold sleeve. Old-style slashes in proclamation sparkle.

Trouser cuffs bloused over the tops of black boots. Communicator grid . . . flip up . . . flip down. A stroll back through the history of Starfleet. A visitation to a rougher time. Halloween.

Feeling as incognito as he had ever felt, Ben Sisko stepped out of his quarters and into commitment. He almost stepped back inside.

Too late—across the corridor, Julian Bashir emerged uneasily from his own quarters, and Sisko got his first full-length view of the twenty-third-century Starfleet uniform. Bashir's black-collared tunic was medical-blue, the trousers black and boots black. Simple. On the left side of his chest was the delta shield insignia, soft gold lined with black, with the circular symbol of the old Sciences Division.

Bashir was staring at Sisko in the same way, scanning Sisko's gold shirt and delta shield, with the command star in the shield instead of the eye.

Sisko could tell they both felt warm and charming about the way they looked, and a little embarrassed.

"Captain," Bashir said, approaching slowly.

Fingering his sleeve slash, Sisko corrected, "Lieutenant, actually. Didn't want to push my luck."

From down the corridor, O'Brien's voice struck up, "Looks good on you, sir."

The two men turned to meet him, and here he came, dressed in a cardinal-red tunic emblazoned with the delta shield and its little mechanical hook signifying Engineering Services, slashed with the rank of ensign on the cuffs, and damned if it *didn't* look good on him, too. There was a cheerful, proclamatory brightness in these uniforms, which broadcast at a glance who these people were, what they did for a living, and what they stood for. The thought occurred that they had to stand for more, and more fiercely, in those tumultuous years.

He gazed at O'Brien as the engineer approached. "Thank you, *Ensign.*"

O'Brien nodded. "Finally got that promotion."

"Wait a minute," Bashir said then. "Aren't you two wearing the wrong colors?"

O'Brien scolded him with a glower. "Don't you know anything about this period?"

Bashir swaggered back a step. "I'm a doctor, not a historian."

Sisko smiled. "In the old days, operations officers wore red, command officers wore gold, and—"

"And women wore less."

They turned at the sound of her voice, and there she was.

A vision of classical womanhood, imperially feminine, and it was at the moment impossible to remember that Jadzia Dax carried within her the lifetimes of several old men.

She wore the red tunic of a female services officer, a thigh-high number—no, higher than that—showing a pair of legs that started in midair and went all the way to the deck. And it was a long, long trip.

Unlike uniforms of their own age, this one had no problems showing off the female figure, and in fact seemed designed to do so. Nothing homogeneous here, no insecurities, no problem with being utterly female.

Dax's dark hair was piled up on her head in some kind of twist, making her seem even taller, and she seemed to be enjoying herself immensely. For a being who had spent much of her existence as various men, she seemed to particularly enjoy being a woman.

Of course with that . . . and those . . .

"What do you think?" she asked, basking in the men's stunned attention and dousing them with a smile.

Sisko parted his lips, but found no voice in there. In

his periphery, O'Brien blinked, then blinked again, as if he couldn't believe what he was seeing.

At Sisko's side, Bashir cleared his throat and croaked, "I think I'm beginning to like history . . ."

The transporter room of *Defiant* was the last stop before vaulting off into the final frontier. And this was a day for grins and stares now that the entire landing party had gathered here.

Worf wore a gaudy turban to conceal his Klingon skull ridge and wore the clothing of a wandering merchant. Odo, whose face merely mocked the humanoid without really being human, was also dressed as a civilian trader. The rest of them looked like a cluster of shore-leavers from a century ago.

Specifically, eighty years ago.

"The original *Enterprise* uses an old-style duotronic sensor array," Miles O'Brien was explaining, finally interested in something other than Dax's uniform. "If we wait for just the right point in the scan cycle, we can decloak the *Defiant* for almost two seconds without being detected."

"Is that enough time to transport us aboard?" Sisko asked.

"Barely."

Dax swept toward them with a padd. "Here are the coordinates. The captain and I will beam to Deck Four and work our way aft. Chief, you and Julian will start your search on Deck Twenty-one."

O'Brien nodded. "And work our way forward."

Sisko turned to Odo and Worf. "What about the station?"

"Little of it is habitable," Worf told him. "Most of *K-Seven* consists of storage area and industrial replication facilities."

Odo added, "It shouldn't take long to search. Security isn't as tight as it is on a starship."

"Remember," Sisko said to them all, "keep contact with people from this time period to a minimum."

He met each of them eye-to-eye, as if to drill home the critical nature of that last instruction.

O'Brien watched his monitor. "We're coming up on a bandshift in the scan cycle."

"Dax," Sisko said, and led the way to the transporter pad.

As he positioned himself properly and turned to face O'Brien and the transport console, he saw on a small monitor behind the engineer the dreamlike image of the beautiful first *Starship Enterprise* angling passively around *Space Station K-Seven.* Its wide main saucer section flickered in the light of the nearest sun, tipped slightly upward as it approached the cloaked *Defiant,* engineering hull swinging below, antimatter pods flickering in foreshortened grace.

What a sight. And he was going there.

He was going there . . .

"Energizing," O'Brien said tightly. "Good luck, sir."

Sisko couldn't muster a response. His tension was souping together with feverish anticipation—was he enjoying himself? Did he dare?

Tampering with time . . . the whole concept was one giant nerve constantly tingling.

He saw Odo, Worf, O'Brien, and Bashir watching as the transporter began humming. They had the same anticipatory tension in their eyes. They were looking forward to this, too, as if muscles were twitching that none could settle. Going back into the past—the real past, not just a holodeck reenactment. Even Odo and Worf shifted uneasily, waiting for their turn. They would be next, transporting to the old space station. O'Brien would key the computer to operate the transporter, and he and Bashir would go to another section of the classic starship.

Strangely, Sisko was suddenly jealous. He wanted to do all three of these searches himself, see all parts of the starship and the station for himself. He wanted to roll back the years and bask awhile in this interesting time.

His crew blurred before his eyes—the transporter effect. The *Defiant* fizzled around him, and he closed his eyes at the last second and drew a breath. The *Enterprise!* A forgotten brightness in the design of starships—bright hull, bright halls, bright uniforms. Nothing muted, all colors declaratively primary. He couldn't wait to see it for real.

When the sizzling sensation on his skin finally breathed away, he opened his eyes, anxious to see the bright corridor he had anticipated.

Nothing. Darkness. He blinked. Still nothing.

Then his eyes began to adjust and he could see only the nightlight glow of a translucent panel in the wall beside him, and the shadowy silhouette of Dax on the other side.

"I thought so," she said.

"What?"

"That the lights in a turbolift go off when no one's inside."

Sisko blinked at her. "You really think about things like that, don't you?"

"All the time." She didn't bother mentioning her elongated life experiences.

Sisko realized that if you live long enough, you think about almost everything eventually. Dax, in another form, had been alive during this time period.

"If I remember," she began, and took hold of one of three angled handles on the lift wall. She twisted it, and a light instantly came on. "Deck Four."

The lift came to life and started moving. Panel lights moved sideways, indicating that the lift was running on a horizontal track. In a moment, it would slow, then shift to a vertical and take them up to Deck Four.

Once there, the lift accommodatingly opened. Ben Sisko and Jadzia Dax stepped out into another age.

The corridor was indeed bright, but not as wide as Sisko had expected. He'd toured a museum ship as a boy, and then thought the corridors were bigger. Of course, he was bigger now.

There were lights and sound, and *lots* of people bustling back and forth. Shipwide communications droned on the shipboard comm system, and crewmen spoke into old-style wall panels. Some wore the same kinds of uniforms as Sisko and Dax, while others wore utility suits or protective overalls. There was even a passing alien dignitary being toured through by an ensign and a yeoman.

Sisko held his breath for a moment, but no one showed any interest in him or Dax. They all had their jobs to do, and this wasn't Toyland. No hobnobbing on duty. Other than a congenial nod from a passing engineer, everybody was too busy to notice a couple of crewmen they didn't know.

Not so unusual. Fraternization between officers and crew wasn't generally encouraged on the battleships of the past centuries. While such policy seemed heartless, there was a crystal-clear reasoning behind it. Emotional attachment could be distracting in times of stress and danger, while loyalty to crewmates in general was preferred. Loyalty was an entirely different commodity than friendship, and could in many ways be more powerful.

"This is so exciting," Dax murmured. "It makes me want to go back to the *Titanic* and make sure they load the boats to capacity this time."

"Mmm," Sisko uttered. "Let's not talk about disasters right now. Don't want to skunk our luck."

She smiled. "Superstition? I didn't think you were the type, Benjamin."

"I'm not. But any sailor who doesn't see a Jonah in the shadows now and then isn't paying attention. Let's start moving."

They moved along the corridor, exchanging stilted nods with other crewmen who all seemed much more purposeful in their strides. Twice Sisko had to jockey sideways to avoid collision, then finally got the hang of bearing to the right with the flow of activity.

"So many people," he muttered.

Dax glanced around as if remembering. "They really packed them in on these old ships."

"And compared to the old ocean-going military ships, starships are practically empty. Do you know that aircraft carriers of the old Earth Navy carried upwards of five thousand men?"

"Including the air wing, yes," she tossed in, just to prove that he couldn't quite get anything on her today. "That's twice the size of the town where I was born."

"You? Jadzia or Dax?"

"Jadzia. Dax was born in a city of two million."

Sisko pointed to a small alcove cut into a corridor wall. "What about over there?"

They ducked into the recession, where panels and drawers allowed access to circuitry and tools with which to work on it, and a ladder into both deck and ceiling provided transport to other decks.

"Perfect," Dax congratulated. "An auxiliary communications juncture."

By "perfect" she meant they couldn't screw things up too badly here.

Sisko opened the drawer she pointed to. "I'll be the repairman. You scan for Darvin."

While he plucked at the circuitry, deliberately not doing anything that would affect any changes, Dax flipped open the top of her old-style tricorder. "You know, I used to have one of these," she murmured nostalgically.

"Mmm-hmm," Sisko responded. "Any sign of Darvin?"

"Not yet," she answered as the tricorder gave off a distinctive sound effect.

"I love these classic mid-twenty-third-century designs," Dax went on softly. "The matte finish, the silver highlights . . . *and* it goes with the uniform."

Dax let the tricorder hang from her shoulder as if modeling a fashion designer's latest evening bag. Sisko stared at her disapprovingly and Dax hastily retrieved the tricorder. "Sorry," she murmured, and resumed scanning.

"I *said* Deck Twenty-one."

Miles O'Brien heard the edge in his voice and agreed wholeheartedly with it. This was the fourth time he'd asked. They'd been standing here for what seemed like hours.

In the dark.

Julian Bashir sighed. Again. "Maybe if you said 'please.'"

"What's wrong with this thing?"

"Don't look at me," Bashir warned. "I don't know *anything* about this time period."

"Maybe it's jammed." Taking the moment for what it was, O'Brien felt around for the circuitry access. "Help me get this wall panel off."

Bashir stepped toward him, but suddenly the turbolift lights popped on. For an instant O'Brien prided himself that the thing was afraid of him and was now deciding to do his bidding, but then the door panels slid open and an *Enterprise* crewman stepped between the two of them.

O'Brien and Bashir made room, trying to look natural, and returned the crewman's nod of greeting. Okay, so this lift was somebody else's trained dog.

The crewman took hold of a stubbed handle angling out of the wall below the light panel. "Deck Fifteen."

Dutifully the lift started moving. O'Brien glanced sheepishly at Bashir, and each reached for one of the other two handles.

O'Brien leaned toward the doctor and mumbled, "I won't tell if you don't."

"Deal."

CHAPTER 5

THE DIAMOND-SHAPED entranceway opened before Odo, admitting him to the *K-Seven* bar. He found the atmosphere most familiar, not terribly unlike Quark's bar on *Deep Space Nine*. Perhaps brighter.

There were people here, lots of them. A bar, a bartender haggling with a persistent salesman, officers, enlisted men, civilians, other merchants and visitors.

Half expecting the people here to notice him and particularly his non-human, non-Klingon, non-anything face, he paused briefly. A few people looked, but none showed interest. Evidently strangers came and went here every day.

He angled toward a group of empty tables in a

corner of the room near the door. Without letting anyone see, he took his tricorder from his pocket and activated it. It had been programmed with Arne Darvin's biodata from the transporter. That, at least, the disguised Klingon had not been able to scramble or crash.

Two senior officers stood at the bar. One was a Vulcan science officer of particularly elegant but relaxed bearing, more relaxed than any Vulcans Odo had ever known. The other officer—the captain!

Odo looked twice to be sure he was seeing correctly. The physical description, the slashes on the sleeves— Captain James Kirk. A man whose name he had heard uttered with both contempt and respect steadily since first becoming involved with Starfleet. A thousand stories were in that man, Odo knew. His interest cranked up a notch.

Sedate in a tapestry-green shirt rather than the expected tan command tunic, James Kirk was a muscular, compact man with quick hazel eyes and a much calmer manner than Odo would've expected, given the legends. Apparently, legend had chosen to reflect only sensational aspects. The crowd neither parted for him nor did he seem to expect such a thing.

Here, today, he was a young James Kirk, in his early thirties and heading toward a starlit career, doing a job for which he was supremely talented. Few people in history had been so right for their jobs as Captain Kirk for his.

The legend cast a long shadow upon Odo and his own time, for he in particular, outcast from another race, would not enjoy the freedoms of the Federation were it not for Starfleet and men like James Kirk. But he managed to keep things in perspective. Many of that young man's great days were yet to come. Restraint must be the order of the day.

Kirk took his drink and turned to lean back on the bar. "Summoning a starship on a Priority-One Channel to guard some storage compartments. Storage compartments of *wheat*."

The Vulcan offered a sympathetic gaze. "Nevertheless, Captain, the Klingons would not enjoy seeing us successfully develop Sherman's Planet."

"I guess not." Kirk clunked his glass back on the bar, drained now, and swung toward Odo.

Odo almost flinched—almost, but realized then that the captain was heading for this door. Before the two officers arrived here, the door opened and two more *Enterprise* officers strolled in—a young dark-haired ensign in Ops gold and an exotic black woman in Services red.

Before they noticed the tricorder, Odo palmed it down and took a seat at the nearest table.

"I see you didn't waste any time taking shore leave," the captain said to the woman.

"And how often do I get shore leave?" she said in a softly low and musical voice.

"She wants to shop, and I thought I would help her," the young man said. He had a thick accent of some brand which Odo couldn't identify.

The door opened again, and this time a portly merchant rumbled in, grinning, and stepped past the officers. "Ah—excuse me, 'scuse me," the man said, catching eyes briefly with as many people as he could. Then he approached the bar and summoned the bartender.

"Mr. Chekov," the captain began. He plucked a small vial from his first officer and handed it to the young ensign. "What do you make of this?"

The ensign took the vial and looked inside. "Ohhh, quadrotriticale! I've read about this, but I've never seen any before."

Exasperated for some reason, the captain grumbled, "Does everybody know about this wheat but me?"

The young man looked up. "Not everyone, Captain. It's a Russian inwention."

"Oh." With a muted sigh, the annoyed captain led his first officer unceremoniously out of the bar.

Odo buried a shudder of relief that they had gone. He knew about captains, leaders. They were always running with sensors on. They could pick up on subtle signals. He didn't know yet whether or not he had been sending any. Was he staring too much? Was his facial mask too alien? How many aliens did this culture know? Would he attract attention by simply being here? Were there regulations he didn't know about and might be violating?

Was there a look in his eye—curiosity, concern, displacement—that the dynamic James Kirk would notice?

The bartender raised his voice then, arguing with

the big merchant. "I don't want any, I told you before, I don't want any more spican flame gems. Thanks to you I already have enough spican flame gems to last me a lifetime."

A brown-haired waitress in a pink outfit approached Odo's table. "What's your pleasure?"

"I'll have a Raktajino," Odo told her, speaking very clearly.

The waitress paused. "You're the second person today who's ordered that. What is it?"

"Surely you want," the merchant at the bar went on, "some Antarian glow water."

Odo kept one ear on the conversation as the bartender sharpened his sales resistance. "I use *that* to polish the flame gems."

"Klingon coffee," he told the waitress. "The second person . . . who was the first?"

"He was an older man. A human."

"Where is he now?" Odo pressed.

"I don't know. He left about an hour ago. He said he might be back. We don't carry any Klingon beverages. Would you like something else?"

"Tarkalean Tea." It didn't matter, since he wasn't going to consume anything.

Now at least he knew he was on the correct trail. An older man—human—asking for a Klingon drink. Even one hundred years back, one plus one was still two.

"You're a difficult man to reach," the merchant at the bar said then, once again attracting Odo's attention. "But I have something from the far reaches of the galaxy!" He plucked into his lapel and pulled out a palm-sized puff of round fur. "Surely you want . . ."

"Not at your price," the bartender drawled.

"Oooh, what is it?" the lady officer asked. "Is it alive? May I hold it?"

The merchant grinned clownishly and placed the puff in the woman's hands.

"Oh, it's adorable! What is it?" She stroked the tiny pink puffball, and as Odo watched and listened, the creature began a soft magnetic purring. . . .

"This ship sure is crowded."

The purr of Bashir's medical tricorder was slightly different from the typical science tricorders O'Brien had handed out to Sisko and Odo. He felt as if there were people all over, all listening as he and Bashir hovered in the corridor of Deck Twenty-one. He had a panel open and was pretending to work while Bashir scanned the general area. They'd had to do one deck at a time, because each deck was sensor shielded to certain intensities. Only the main sensor system of the ship itself could scan through the decks. A hand-held tricorder just couldn't.

He reached for the panel, fingered the circuits, then retreated. This had gone on for fifteen minutes now. Hand in, hand out. Don't touch anything.

"Moments like this, I wonder why I ever left home," he muttered after three security officers passed by a little too closely for comfort.

"Your old granny's garden-moated bungalow in Ireland?" Bashir asked distractedly as he scanned.

O'Brien humphed. "My old granny lives in a condo in Miami. She's a real estate broker. Claims to have sold the Blarney Stone half a dozen times and the Atlantic Ocean twice."

He sighed again and stared at the circuit box, frustrated. Who had put this ship together this way? This certainly wasn't the original design, yet there was a strange reasoning behind the alterations he could decipher. They were reworked for added power and for simplicity, but he couldn't tell which was which unless he pulled them apart. He'd tried twice, and twice he'd been wrong. His hands clenched and fidgeted at his sides. How could he pretend to work on something he was afraid to bungle? He dared not leave a mechanical trail or do something that might compromise the ship's action, even in the months to come. That would change the future, too—

"Chief," the doctor said, "you're supposed to be working."

"I'm afraid to touch anything! It's all cross-circuited and patched together. I can't make heads or tails of it!"

"Sounds like one of your repair jobs."

Prodded by the doctor's tease, O'Brien stuck his hand into the panel again and tried to pretend that he was doing something.

"No sign of Darvin in this section," Bashir said quietly. "I'm going to widen the scan radius." He opened the panel on the unfamiliar tricorder. "If I can figure out how . . ."

"Keep the scan field below twenty milliwatts," O'Brien warned. "Otherwise you'll set off the ship's internal sensors."

Bashir rolled his eyes. "Thank you, Chief. I *was* listening at the mission briefing."

"Thought maybe you dozed off as usual."

"What are you two doing here?" A strange voice lanced between them and O'Brien knew he visibly flinched.

He spun around, looking guilty.

A fresh-faced engineer had cornered them— lieutenant, j.g. He carried one of the old trident scanners and seemed surprised, maybe shocked, to see O'Brien with his hands in the pie closet.

"Scotty told *me* to do this," the lieutenant said.

O'Brien stared. He had no idea what "this" meant. "Oh—oh, *you* were going to do this . . ."

The lieutenant tipped his head. "It's on the duty roster."

There must've been a dozen things to say, but O'Brien couldn't think of a single one. Not a one.

"Must've been a mix-up," Bashir filled in affably.

Unfortunately, that brought the engineer's attention to a doctor standing around the engineering decks without anybody to treat.

"Isn't that a medical tricorder?" the young man asked.

Bashir looked down at the device in his hand as if

he'd just discovered it there. "Yes. Yes, it is. I'm a doctor."

The lieutenant looked more puzzled. "Why do we need a doctor to repair a power relay?"

O'Brien swung to Bashir and gave him the same look, as if he had no idea either. Bashir didn't seem to appreciate that.

"You don't," Bashir said. "Obviously. I was doing a study . . . it has to do with work-related stress."

"Oh," the engineer responded. He wasn't suspicious at all, despite their bizarre stumbling. Apparently he had no reason—no, of course, he didn't—to believe there would be anything going on. After all, both men were dressed as crewmen of this ship and that's all. There was no reason for every neck hair to be standing. No reason at all.

"You two go on," Bashir encouraged, getting in his revenge on O'Brien. "Pretend I'm not even here."

Feeling like a smokestack about to blow, O'Brien smeared the doctor with a dirty look, dirty enough that Bashir turned back to his bioscan.

The young engineer joined O'Brien at the panel. "So where should we start?"

In granny's bungalow. "Well . . . obviously . . . the first thing to do is take this transtator here and . . ."

O'Brien tugged the transtator from its socket and it thanked him with a scolding *zap* across the ends of his fingers. Half the lights in the corridor went dim and the whole deck's power grid started ebbing and moaning.

He put the thing back.

"And leave it right where it is." He sighed.

The engineer peered at him as if looking into a funhouse mirror, unsure of what he was seeing.

O'Brien stepped back and was two seconds from running off at the mouth about coming back in time and chasing Klingons who were disguised as humans and really working on a space station a hell of a long way from here near a planet nobody had discovered yet, when Bashir stepped in and took him by the arm.

"The job pressure's been getting to him," the doctor explained, leaning conspiratorially toward the young lieutenant. "Why don't you take over?" The engineer nodded sympathetically, and Bashir tugged on O'Brien. "All right, Ensign, I think I've seen enough. Let's get you back to Sickbay."

And put you back in your straitjacket.

O'Brien glowered at him but was glad enough to have a way out of this. He offered his most puppyish look to the other engineer and acted as if he'd just pulled his trousers on after being caught without them. "I'd appreciate it if you didn't mention this to anyone . . ."

"No problem," the engineer said with annoying gentility. "Hope you feel better."

A little groan of frustration garbled up in O'Brien's throat. "Thanks."

He and Bashir moved away down the corridor, with Bashir ushering him custodially.

"Isn't this nice?" Bashir murmured. "Now you

have a reputation on the classic *Enterprise* as being a stressed-out incompetent."

O'Brien inhaled sharply, then couldn't get it all out. "Lovely!"

Odo sat at his table and ignored the tea which had been served to him. The idea of participating at all in this era frightened him. The smallest change could mean ruination eighty years from now, and he was determined such catastrophe would not be his fault.

It did smell good, though. Perhaps just a sip or two.

He felt somewhat more content and peaceful now than he had when he first came in. Strange how much more at home he felt now . . . *am I smiling?*

The diamond-shaped door whispered open and Odo raised his eyes. Worf stood at the entranceway, scanning the bar. He still looked like a Klingon to Odo, even with the turban and civilian clothing, but not to all these other people.

Worf spotted Odo and instantly angled toward him, joining him on the other side of the table. He glanced around the bar briefly to be sure no one was close enough to hear, as if anyone cared, then leaned forward a little. "I have completed my search of the primary habitat level and . . ."

His voice trailed off as another sound bubbled between them. He frowned and shivered.

"What was that sound?" he asked.

"Soothing, isn't it?" Odo suggested. "The bartender called it a . . . a . . ."

But Worf bolted to his feet as Odo raised the puff ball of fur he had been holding in his lap.

Instantly the little animal's purring and cooing turned to squeals of alarm and it began quivering violently in Odo's hand.

No doubt about the cause—

Worf shoved to his feet, his chair flying out behind him. He stumbled backward in revulsion.

Odo yanked his pet back and tried to calm it.

Worf glared and scowled.

"A tribble!"

CHAPTER
6

"EVERYTHING ALL RIGHT over here?"

The waitress rushed over with an expression on her face that told Odo she sensed trouble between two patrons who looked as if they came from far, far apart.

Worf was still glaring at the round puff in Odo's hands. To the waitress he ground out, "We . . . are . . . fine."

"Sit down," Odo said to Worf as the waitress moved away. "You're drawing attention."

Slowly and very unhappily, Worf took his seat once again, but did not shift toward the table. The tribble in Odo's hand stopped screaming, but did shudder and flinch repeatedly.

"Where did you get that thing?" Worf demanded.

"From a man named Cyrano Jones. He said tribbles like everyone, but it doesn't seem to like you," Odo commented with mild interest.

"The feeling is mutual," Worf rumbled. "Tribbles are . . . detestable creatures."

"Interesting," Odo said. "It's my experience that most humanoids love soft furry animals." He ran his hand along the ball of fuzz and was lost again in the creature's gentle cooing. "Especially if they make a pleasing sound . . ."

"They do nothing but consume food and breed," Worf uttered with contempt. "If you feed that thing more than the smallest morsel, within a few hours you will have ten tribbles. Then a hundred. Then a thousand!"

"Calm down."

"They were once considered mortal enemies of the Klingon Empire."

With unshielded mockery, Odo looked up at him and held the tribble higher. *"This* is a mortal enemy of the Klingon Empire?"

"They were an ecological menace! A scourge! A plague that had to be wiped out!"

"Wiped out? What are you saying?"

With relish, Worf actually inched forward. "The Empire sent an entire armada to obliterate the tribble homeworld. Then hundreds of handpicked warriors were dispatched to track them down and destroy them throughout the galaxy. By the end of the twenty-third century, they were completely eradicated!"

With a groan, Odo parried, "Another glorious

chapter in Klingon history. Tell me, do they still sing songs about the Great Tribble Hunt?"

Worf's face crumpled, not exactly with embarrassment but with some mixture of that and frustration at Odo's lack of comprehension about the critical nature of eradicating purring fuzzballs.

He parted his lips to speak, but the station broke into red alert. Klaxons blared all over, in the bar and in the corridor.

Most patrons in the bar gawked and swiveled, not knowing what to do. The Starfleet personnel, though, in sharp contrast, all bolted for the door.

Worf and Odo were among those who swiveled and gawked.

"Bureaucrats. Summoning a ship of the line as if calling a moon shuttle. Never ceases to amaze me. Put a collar and a badge on a civilian, and he turns into a commandant."

Aware that he was grumbling, Kirk pulled his cup of coffee out of the access port in the bulkhead and turned toward Spock. They were in one of the ship's briefing rooms, only because Kirk had wanted a few moments to grumble in peace.

"Maybe I'm a snob, Mr. Spock," he went on obsessively. "I just expect a person to have a few experiences under his belt before he starts giving orders to people who actually have some. My crew deserves better than to be treated like hired help."

"Agreed," Spock said impassively, but Kirk knew his first officer was only placating him.

Spock was a steadying presence for him, both in times of tension and in times of prickly annoyance, like now. Like a brick in the sand, Spock seldom flinched, no matter how the winds rattled the stuff around him. Right now the Vulcan was amused. Though there was little outward hint, Kirk could tell. A twinkle in the black-dot eyes, the way Spock's Vulcan brows both went up at the same time, and just a mist of a smile, very subdued. Amused, for sure. Somehow, it helped.

He blew across the top of his coffee and took a sip. "We're not at the beck and call of every administrator who can't tell the difference between a security detail and a fully rigged and armed starship. You don't summon four hundred and thirty people to do the job of two."

"Mr. Barris would prefer to have many more than two guards," Spock observed, standing nearby with a profound economy of movement.

"Times like this," Kirk grumbled on, "I wish I could retire to some barrier island someplace, get myself a little wooden ship with a narrow hull and a deep grip on the water and go cantering around the seaways . . . spearing bureaucrats with my bowsprit."

He gritted his teeth over the last words. Felt good. Then he imagined it. Looked even better. Shish-kebabed Barris.

The comm on the table whistled. Fielding Spock's bemused gaze, Kirk turned and punched the button. "Yes, what is it?

"Message from Starfleet, Captain, priority channel. Admiral Fitzpatrick speaking."

"Put it on visual, Lieutenant."

On the small centerpiece screen, a frosty man in a gold shirt appeared. *"Captain Kirk."*

"Kirk here."

"Captain, it is not necessary to remind you of the importance to the Federation of Sherman's Planet. The key to our winning of this planet is the grain quadrotriticale. The shipment of it must be protected."

Kirk looked at Spock with unshielded annoyance, and Spock's only response was to passively fold his arms. It was his equivalent of sighing and leaning on a wall without really doing either.

"Effective immediately," the admiral went on, *"you will render any aid and assistance which Secretary Barris may require. The safety of the grain and the project are your responsibility."*

From exploration and defense to babysitting wheat in one drumming boom.

"Well, that's just . . . lovely," Kirk complained.

Spock nodded. "But not totally unexpected."

No, it wasn't. Kirk knew Fitzpatrick and had never given him a serious thought. Whenever circumstances had required him to respect Fitzpatrick, he had been respecting the uniform and not the man. A terminally office-bound serviceman, Fitzpatrick had never commanded anything bigger than a bathtub and no farther afield than Starfleet Academy. He was a paper admiral, running paper battles in a paper universe.

DIANE CAREY

Now he was communicating with another paper-pusher—Barris.

Between the two, instead of pushing paper, they were pushing a starship.

The comm whistled again. *"Captain Kirk, Captain Kirk!"*

"Yes, Lieutenant, what is it?"

"Sensors are picking up a Klingon battlecruiser, rapidly closing on the station!"

"Go to red alert. Notify Mr. Lurry. We'll be right up."

Red alert trumpeted throughout the decks of the *Starship Enterprise.* On the bulkheads, light panels slashed on and off in bright carnelian alarm, making sure that nobody heard wrong. This was not yellow alert.

A voice on the comm system boomed, *"Red alert. Red alert. All hands to battle stations. This is not a drill."*

Ben Sisko looked at Dax, and she looked back. For the first time, she seemed confused.

"What should we do?" she asked. All around them other crew members—real ones—hurried about, heading for assigned emergency postings. For each of these people there was a deck assignment and a station bill made up by that deck's officer of the watch, and on that station bill was a place to go during an emergency. A job to do. Something very specific. Go there, stand by.

Sisko glanced around. "Get to battle stations."

He closed up the panel he was pretending to fuss with, and the two of them plunged into the hustling crowd, trying to blend in and hoping they didn't end up stampeded into a place where they couldn't explain themselves.

To avoid any embarrassment—or worse, the chance of being discovered—Sisko ducked into a turbolift and waited for Dax to join him. He grasped the handle then and said, "Deck Seven."

The lift started whirring, and Sisko gave it a few seconds to get between decks. Then he twisted the handle to *off,* let go of the handle and the lift stopped.

"Let's see if we can find out what's going on," he said. He tapped his uniform insignia. "Sisko to *Defiant.*"

He waited for a response, long enough that Dax started grinning in that you're-being-an-idiot way she had. Funny—the one trait she had left over from her days as Curzon Dax, and it had to be that.

Sisko sighed with annoyance, realizing his mistake, and pulled out the communicator stuck to the back of his belt. Those were the days.

He flipped the grid open. "Sisko to *Defiant.*"

"Defiant here." It was Kira.

Sisko knew she'd been working on making the Orb operate, but now she was on the bridge and answering for the ship. That alone meant something was going on.

"The *Enterprise* just went to red alert. What's going on out there?"

"A Klingon D-Seven battlecruiser has dropped out of warp and is approaching the station."

"Are they locking weapons?"

"Not yet."

Dax held out a hand, as if remembering. "Wait a minute . . . Kira, can you identify the Klingon ship?"

There was silence for a few working seconds on board the *Defiant,* then Kira's voice returned, *"The IKS Gr'oth."*

Dax smiled conspiratorially. "That's Koloth's ship!"

Grinding her with a glare, Sisko decided she was enjoying herself way too much.

"Curzon's old friend?" he guessed.

"Yes, and he's not going to attack. I remember Koloth telling me he once traded insults with Kirk on a space station near the Federation border. He always regretted not getting a chance to face him in battle."

Kira's voice broke in. *"The Klingon ship just transported two people over to the station manager's office, Captain."*

"That's Koloth!" Dax exclaimed, gathering memories and plugging them into the moment. "Maybe we should beam over to the station and help Odo and Worf. We know that Darvin was there a few hours ago and—"

"I think," Sisko said evenly, "maybe Dr. Bashir and Chief O'Brien should go."

"But if we went, we might run into Koloth!"

"Exactly."

Dax huffed with frustration that he wasn't letting

her have any fun. "It's not as if he'd recognize me!
And I'd love to see him in his prime—"

"Dax," Sisko said sternly. Then into the communicator he said, "Major, beam the doctor and the chief
over to K-Seven."

"Aye, sir."

Sisko clapped the communicator shut and grasped
the lift handle.

"It would've been fun," Dax complained.

He leered at her. "Too much fun."

The corridors of the *Enterprise* bristled with activity under red alert. The constant whooping of the
alarms kept adrenaline flowing. As he and Spock
hurried to the nearest turbolift, Kirk was gratified by
the excitement he felt in the crewmen rushing past
them. His crew liked action, even battle. They were
that kind of people. They had to like it even while
disdaining it. That was the only way to survive.

When the lift reached the topmost deck of the
starship and the doors parted, the comforting sounds
of the bridge engulfed Kirk like a blanket. All his
nerves buzzing, Kirk dropped to the lower deck and
came around his command chair, settled into it, and
immediately asked, "What is the position of the
Klingon ship?"

As Spock came to stand beside him, Chekov answered, "Hundred kilometers off K-Seven. It's just
sitting there."

"Captain," Uhura said then, "I have Mr. Lurry."

"Put him on visual."

"Aye, sir."

When the picture of Lurry appeared, seated and calm, Kirk quickly told him, "Mr. Lurry, there's a Klingon warship hanging one hundred kilometers off your station."

"I don't think the Klingons are planning to attack us."

"Why not?"

"Because at this moment the captain of the Klingon ship is sitting right here in my office."

Lurry doctored the sensor visual to expand the picture, showing a Klingon commander and his first officer, both glaring defiantly into the screen.

Koloth. Hand on his knee, legs crossed. Doing his imitation of a persnickety winner. Even though he hadn't won anything yet. Or lately, for that matter.

Then again, he was down there in the office and Kirk was up here, about to have to walk in there as if summoned.

"Cancel red alert," Kirk growled. "We'll beam right down."

"Of all Klingons, it has to be Koloth."

Jim Kirk strode out of the *Enterprise*'s transporter room and felt like taking a shower. He'd just met with and sparred with Captain Koloth in Manager Lurry's office.

"Is there something specific about Captain Koloth which disturbs you?" Spock asked, as they walked the corridor.

"Nothing specific," Kirk admitted. "Attitude,

mostly. Undeserved arrogance. He's never done any-thing remarkable, but he feels he can fly into Federa-tion border territory and demand shore leave on a Federation-run station."

"You gave it to him," Spock pointed out.

Kirk sighed. "I said that, didn't I? The sailor in me was empathizing with their having been in space for five months without a break. I should've told them to turn around and eat asteroids. Let's go this way," he added, suddenly turning down the corridor that led toward the mess hall and rec room.

"Are you hungry, sir?" Spock asked.

"The corridor's empty. The watch is probably finishing lunch. I feel like seeing them."

Spock nodded as if he understood, but Kirk knew he probably didn't.

Then again, maybe he did.

"Lurry, Barris, Koloth," Kirk muttered, as he fixed on the rec room door panel and went through it.

The first person he saw was Chief Engineer Mont-gomery Scott, nested at a computer terminal, gazing happily into the screen as if looking at a picture of a beautiful woman.

Kirk leaned forward, enough to catch a glimpse of the screen, hoping for a glimpse of paradise. No such luck.

"Another technical journal, Scotty?" he asked. "Don't you ever relax?"

The engineer blinked up at him, confused. "I *am* relaxing!"

Just that small exchange, a venture into normalcy

after this peculiar morning, set Kirk on the road to feeling better.

He strode to the largest table, where a dozen of his crew were gathered over a purring mass of powder puffs. What was this?

The powder puffs were purring, and the crew was petting them. Alive?

He glanced across the table to where Ship's Chief Surgeon Leonard McCoy stood with his arms folded, gazing down at the puff balls. Well, there wasn't any contamination or risk, then, because McCoy would've isolated the little puffs by now. Instead, the doctor seemed fascinated by the effect of the purring on the crew members. Everyone was completely quiet, mesmerized by the soft noise and the action of stroking what amounted to an earless, legless, faceless bunny.

"How long have you had that thing, Lieutenant?" McCoy asked.

Lieutenant Uhura glanced up at McCoy. "Since yesterday, Doctor. This morning I found out that he—I mean, she—had had babies."

"Well, in that case I'd say you got a bargain."

"You running a nursery, Lieutenant?" Kirk asked.

"Oh, Captain," she said, just noticing that he was there. "I hadn't intended to, sir, but the tribble had other plans."

As the mesmerized crew drowsily stroked the dozen tribbles on the table, Spock picked up a white fuzz ball and put it to his ear. It purred and bubbled happily.

Kirk looked at Uhura. "Did you get this at the space station?"

"Yes, sir."

"A most curious creature, Captain," Spock observed. At first, he was listening to the tribble, tugging its fur analytically, feeling the consistency of its body, but after a few seconds, he began simply stroking it groggily. "Its trilling seems to have a tranquilizing effect on the human nervous system. Fortunately, of course, I am . . . immune . . . to its . . . effect . . ."

Kirk felt his tensions untwist a little as he embarrassed Spock with a quirky gaze.

Spock realized what was happening, glanced at Uhura, at Lieutenant Freeman, finally at Kirk, and deposited his tribble back on the table.

Stifling a comment—he'd store it up for later—Kirk simply led the way out of the rec room.

Lurry, Barris, Koloth, Tribbles.

CHAPTER 7

"I MAY BE SICK . . ."

The two time cops stared at Sisko with expressions so much alike that he wasn't sure which one was about to throw up on his desk. He held his breath for a moment, ready to dodge away in either direction.

"Tell me about it," Lucsly said then. "My palms are sweating."

Dulmur swallowed hard. "Think of the repercussions . . . a Klingon from the twenty-third century realizes that a Federation vessel from the future is potentially within his grasp . . ."

"We'd all be speaking Klingonese," the other one said.

"Can you imagine?" Dulmur looked at him. "All those consonants."

"Q'apla," Lucsly parried, then they both shuddered.

"I didn't let Dax go," Sisko told them soothingly. "Koloth never knew we were even there."

"We'll be the judge of that," Lucsly told him.

"What happened next?" Dulmur asked bluntly.

Beginning to get the idea that he was being interviewed by two guys with the sense of humor of customs officials, Sisko sighed. "It was one thing to convince Dax to stay out of history's way. The problem was, history had a funny habit of coming *our* way."

"Benjamin . . . look."

The corridor was quiet now, all hands at stations or at lunch, except for Ben Sisko and Jadzia Dax, who were still desperately pretending to be doing something while scanning for a single renegade old Klingon. They hadn't found Darvin yet, but they did find destiny strolling down upon them as Ben Sisko looked up into the face of legend.

Faces—two.

Down the empty corridor strode two officers, conversing casually and seeming eminently at home here in these crisp halls.

Sisko turned his back until he could see the two only in his periphery, and tried to look occupied.

But he was listening as the wall comm whistled and the two officers angled toward it.

"Bridge to Captain Kirk," came a voice with an accent.

The young officer in the patina-green shirt tapped the wall comm. "Kirk here."

His voice was . . . well, commanding. It gave Sisko a shiver of proximity. He was within steps of the real thing, one of the first men to expand the Federation's influence in the settled galaxy. James Kirk was one of the early propellants pushing the envelope of civilization. He had a reputation for impulse and sideswiping, something Sisko understood from these past years as commander of an outpost on the deep frontier. History both cherished and disdained James Kirk—cherished for his unflagging energy and sense of right and wrong, disdained for his propensity to meddle and his rattlesnake tenacity at taking things into his own hands. He was a man who would load his dice if he could, and it took special taste to appreciate that.

But historians were documenters and analysts, not captains. Sisko always considered such caveats, and read between the lines.

Beside Kirk was the other half of the legend—Commander Spock. Still alive somewhere in Sisko's time, this Vulcan had been the first of his kind to break the cultural barriers and join Starfleet. It had cost him his relationship with his father for a couple of decades, but he stuck to his commitment as an officer.

The voice from the bridge said, *"Mr. Barris is waiting on Channel A to speak to you, sir."*

Kirk's posture tightened. "Pipe it down here, Mr. Chekov."

"Aye, sir. Mr. Barris is coming on."

"Keep working," Sisko murmured to Dax. "We're just a regular maintenance crew doing our job . . ."

"Yes, Mr. Barris, what can I do for you?"

"Kirk! This station is swarming with Klingons!"

Kirk fixed his eyes on his Vulcan first officer and patronized his way through the comm unit. "I was not aware, Mr. Barris, that twelve Klingons constitutes a swarm."

"Captain Kirk, there are Klingon soldiers on this station. Now, I want you to keep that grain safe!"

Sisko stiffened, anticipating.

Dax giggled, then tried to suppress it.

Sisko growled, "Dax . . ."

"I had no idea," she murmured.

"What?"

"He's so much more handsome in person . . . and those eyes . . ."

Continuing to pretend work, Sisko dismissed, "Kirk had quite the reputation as a ladies' man."

"Not him," Dax corrected, eyeing the pair. "Spock."

Sisko glanced at the Vulcan and couldn't deny Dax's assessment. Commander Spock possessed a passive elegance ideal to his position as second in command and foil to Captain Kirk. The two were as opposite as two men could be, physically but also in manner. As such they seemed an almost perfect set.

Kirk folded his arms. "Mr. Barris," he went on, "I have guards around the grain, I have guards around the Klingons . . . those guards are there because Starfleet wants them there. As for what *you* want—"

Sisko braced himself for a show, but Kirk glanced at Spock, and the restraint of his first officer seemed to scold him down.

"It has been noted and logged," the captain concluded with an edge.

Enthralled, Dax was looking too much.

Clapping the panel shut, Sisko straightened. "Let's go."

"Now?" she protested.

"Now."

He urged her around the corner, out of line of sight, then paused and listened as Spock's low voice traveled around to them.

"Captain, may I ask where you'll be?"

"Sickbay. With a . . . headache."

As the captain rounded the corner and headed away, Dax took one last peek. "I can't believe you don't want to at least *meet* Kirk!" she said.

"That's the last thing on my mind," Sisko said flatly.

She leaned toward him. "Come on, Benjamin. Are you telling me that you're not the tiniest bit interested in meeting one of the most famous men in Starfleet history?"

"We have a job to do."

"But that's James Kirk," she insisted right past his stern expression.

"Look," he protested, "of course I'd like to meet

him. I'd like to shake his hand and ask him about . . . fighting the Gorn on Cestus Three. But that's not why we're here, old man."

"You're right," Dax said as he drew her along. "I guess the difference between you and me is that I remember this time. I lived in this time." She glanced back the way they'd come. "It's hard not to want to be part of it again."

Kirk paced into sickbay, all his tensions wired back up just from hearing Nils Barris's voice.

"Hi, Jim," McCoy said casually, putting a restraining beaker on top of a whole clutch of tribbles.

"Bones," Kirk returned. "What've you got for a headache?"

McCoy looked up at him in a kind of delight. "Let me guess. The Klingons. Barris!"

"Both." Kirk looked down at the tribbles in the big beaker. "How many of these did Uhura give you?"

"Just one."

"But you've got . . . uh, eleven."

"Noticed that, uh? Here. This ought to take care of it." The doctor handed him a couple of pills.

Accepting the pills, Kirk started adding up the minutes since he'd seen Uhura and her tribbles in the rec room. These looked almost full grown.

He pointed at them. "How do they . . . how do they . . ."

McCoy held out a defensive hand. "I haven't figured that out yet. But I can tell you this much—

almost fifty percent of the creature's metabolism is geared toward reproduction." The doctor leaned on the table and peered at Kirk. "Do you know what you get if you feed a tribble too much?"

Simmering, Kirk peered back. "A fat tribble."

Annoyed that he was going to have to say it outright, McCoy told him, "No, you get a whole bunch of hungry little tribbles."

"Well, Bones, all I can suggest," Kirk told him, heading toward the door, "is that you open up a maternity ward."

Leonard McCoy watched the captain leave and regretted not being able to come up with a snide remark. He knew there was some problem with these tribbles, but damned if he couldn't find it. They were soft, they made a pretty noise, they were nice, they were passive, they liked being held close, and they made more little puff balls to love and purr. Quickly. Something about this didn't add up.

Still, the sickbay sounded kind of pleasant with eleven tribbles cooing in it.

The door panel slid open again and for a moment he thought the captain might be coming back, but when he looked up, he saw a young science officer whom he didn't know. The young man was of slender build and dark features.

"Oh—I'm so sorry," the young man said when he saw McCoy. Educated in England. "I thought everyone was at lunch, sir."

"We always keep at least one person on watch in all

departments," McCoy said. How come this man didn't know that? "Do I know you?"

"Um . . . no, sir, I don't believe so. I just came aboard. I'm only visiting. I should've reported to you, but with all the alerts—"

"Visiting? From the station? You're a Starfleet officer. I didn't know there were any of us on the station."

"Uh . . . no, there aren't, sir. I just came on board recently, for transport to my new assignment."

Pretty vague, but McCoy didn't care about the details. "You a doctor? Or are you sick?"

"Pardon me," the young man said, extending his hand to McCoy. "Dr. Julian Bashir, sir. I'm doing a study on systems-wide medical sensor functions and I thought I'd have a look about the sickbay."

"What's that study for?"

"Oh, someone at Starfleet wants to enhance the capability of tracking individuals by biotechnics. It's for use on stations like K-Seven and for . . . oh, for instance, tracking down disguised spies on ships."

McCoy harrumphed at the idea. "Sounds like something Starfleet Medical would come up with to keep people busy."

"Very likely," Bashir said with a tolerant and perhaps nervous smile. "About the ship-wide sensors . . . do you think they could pick up an individual by biotechniques? Say a Vulcan or a . . . oh, a Klingon?"

"Well, we'd have to do a deck-by-deck scan,"

McCoy told him. "Klingons aren't that hard to detect. They hate to shave, for one. They don't like our food, for another."

"Doctor," Bashir said with a tuck of his chin, "are you teasing me?"

"A little. It's just a muscle reaction from not having a Vulcan around. Why don't you have some coffee and set yourself up at that terminal over there. The computer'll assist you with your sensor research. I'll clear it with the bridge."

The other doctor, luckily, was engrossed in his study of the little clutch of furballs when Bashir's communicator let out one plaintive bleep—and he turned quickly to see whether or not McCoy had noticed, but no. The bleep blended in with the trill and purr of those little animals.

Bashir turned and headed back for the door. "I forgot something. Back soon, sir."

McCoy didn't even look up. "Mmm-hmm."

The corridor was bright and bustling, but no one noticed him as he headed around a corner, trying to find a place where he could use the communicator without anyone listening. Suddenly a hand reached out and yanked him into an alcove. It was O'Brien, holding his own communicator.

"The next bandshift in the Enterprise *scan cycle will be in three minutes,"* Major Kira's voice flickered over the old-style device.

"We'll be ready, Major. O'Brien out."

Bashir got the idea quickly enough—they'd been

ordered out of here for now. They'd be beaming out. That meant privacy. "We'd better get to a turbolift."

Together they turned and headed for the nearest lift, then had to wait as the lift came to their deck. When it did, the doors slid open and they boarded, but couldn't beam out.

Standing in the lift, a young woman looked at them both, and Bashir remembered her—he'd seen her before. He'd even spoken to her, though he didn't recall specifically when. She hadn't made much of an impression, and he was dismayed to find he'd made one on her.

"Hello, again," the young lieutenant said.

"Hello," Bashir responded automatically.

O'Brien took the lift's control. "Deck Ten."

The woman looked down at Bashir's waist. "Your flap's open."

He blinked. "Excuse me?"

"On your tricorder. You're draining power."

He looked down at the tricorder—he'd forgotten he was still carrying it. Sure enough, the front flap was hanging open. He snapped it closed. "Oh—thank you."

"He's always doing that," O'Brien teased.

She smiled at him. "I'm coming in to the sickbay tomorrow for my physical . . . fifteen hundred. Lieutenant Watley."

The lift doors opened and she started out, but then she turned in the doorway so the door panels wouldn't close and smiled again, this time infectiously.

Bashir smiled back. Maybe he could arrange to be in sickbay about fifteen hundred tomorrow. Maybe.

She sidled away with a last glance, and O'Brien said, "You realize, of course, she was only using you to get to me."

The lift doors closed. O'Brien activated it, made it go between decks, then stopped it.

"Watley," Bashir said, his chest suddenly constricting. "That was my great-grandmother's name!"

"Funny," the engineer drawled as he pulled out his communicator again.

"I think she was in Starfleet!"

O'Brien scolded him with a glower about not knowing his family history any better than that, then said, "It's a common name."

"But what if that was her!" Bashir's mind raced.

"Do you realize the odds?" The engineer quickly fingered the controls of the communicator.

Bashir waved a panicked hand. "No one ever met my great-grandfather—this could be a predestinational paradox!" As O'Brien shook his head, the doctor insisted, "Didn't you take elementary temporal mechanics at the Academy? I may be destined to fall in love with that woman and . . . and become my own great-grandfather!"

O'Brien stared. "You're being ridiculous."

"Ridiculous? If I don't meet with her tomorrow, I may never be born!"

Kira's voice trickled through the communicator in the nick of time. *"Chief, are you ready for transport?"*

"Are we ever," O'Brien said.

"Stand by."

"You saw the way she looked at me?" Bashir obsessed, frantically imagining all the repercussions of his life, the people he'd saved who would now die, the tests he'd conducted that would go unsolved, and by the time the thought spread itself to its full potential, the entire universe was collapsing upon itself because he'd never been born. He caught O'Brien's look again and added, "You can't just dismiss this!"

"I can try."

"Fine!" Bashir insisted as the tingling rush of the transporter effect shivered all his skin hairs. "But I can't wait to see your face when you get back to DS9 and find out I never existed!"

CHAPTER
8

MILES O'BRIEN LED the way into the bar on Deep Space Station K-Seven. This place was like the ship—much brighter than anything they were used to. And over there were Odo and Worf, at a table just past two other tables, which were crowded with several *Enterprise* crewmen and another surly dark-haired group in matching silver tunics with black shirts underneath. Probably a crew from some other division.

O'Brien and Bashir crossed the room to Odo and Worf, and O'Brien couldn't help feeling a bit odd—he caught the glances of the other table of Starfleet crew, who were probably wondering why he and the doctor were joining a pair of civilian traders instead of other Starfleeters.

Well, some chips had to fall, anyway.

"Chief," Bashir said, as the two of them joined Odo and Worf, "clearly we've been going about this search business all wrong."

"You're right, Julian," O'Brien fell in. "Why bother manually searching thirty decks when you can just plunk yourself down at a bar and wait for Darvin to come to you."

"We have *reason* to believe," Odo bristled instantly, "that Darvin will return to this area."

"Ah, yes," O'Brien prodded. "For his raktajino."

Bashir quickly added, "A vital clue others might have missed. How fortunate that vital clue has kept you glued to this bar for the past three hours—having drinks—while we're crawling through conduits."

As they sat down, the ribbing was interrupted when the door panel parted again and three more Starfleet personnel came through. O'Brien automatically looked, knowing they were indeed searching for someone who, in the large scheme, might come wandering back in here.

"My God," he croaked, as he stared at the three Starfleet officers who had just entered. "There he is!"

At the door were three officers, two in gold and one in red. The red-shirt was a man of medium build with dark hair, but that wasn't what caught his attention. One of the gold-shirts was very young with relatively long dark hair for the era, but that also wasn't what caught O'Brien.

"Who?" Bashir asked.

Leaning a little toward him, O'Brien continued staring at the third man. *"Kirk!"*

"Where?" Worf craned to see past his crewmates.

The three Starfleet officers strode in, glanced at the table full of silver-tunicked men, then took a table of their own.

"Right there," O'Brien whispered anxiously. "He's just sitting those other two guys! The one in gold, on the left."

"That's Kirk?" Bashir asked.

"Look at him! The way he walks . . . that glint of command in his eye . . . that's him, all right!"

His hands quivered as the piece of history took a seat mere paces from him. He wanted desperately to clamber over there like a starstruck kid and ask for James Kirk's autograph. The dubious looks in Bashir's and Odo's eyes annoyed him. Of course that was Kirk! The sandy hair, the tall stature, the muscles, the strong expression . . . of course, it was Kirk.

"It would be an honor to meet him," Worf said.

"Let's buy him a drink!" O'Brien gushed.

"Gentlemen," Odo drew up. "No one's buying anyone drinks."

Glancing at Worf, O'Brien took the scolding with a blush. "He's right. We can't risk altering the timeline."

At the bar, one of the men in silver and black poured a drink for a jovial merchant, and with great dripping contempt he asked, "The Earthers like those fuzzy things, don't they?"

"Well, yes!" The merchant chuckled nervously, then took a drink of what had been poured.

"Well, frankly, I never liked Earthers. They remind

me of Regulan bloodworms," the bearded man said, directing his comment right at the three Starfleeters who had just come in. This antagonist had drunk too much and was giving in to the tensions already flowing in the bar. The urge to pick on humans.

O'Brien had seen it before.

"No!" the bearded man howled over the laughter of his own crewmates. "I just remembered! There *is* one Earth man who doesn't remind me of a Regulan bloodworm. That's Kirk!"

He sidled between the chairs to just outside of kicking distance from the three newcomers.

O'Brien felt his hand start to tremble. Insulting Captain Kirk! While Kirk was sitting right there! He started to wonder how much it would wreck the timeline if he just beat a little of the hell out of a few people. He looked around to see what others were thinking—the *Enterprise* crewmen were boiling in their seats, but no one moved much. In fact, they didn't move at all. They all looked frozen to their places by their very anger.

And so was he.

"A Regulan bloodworm is soft," the antagonist went on, "and shapeless. But Kirk isn't soft. Kirk may be a swaggering dictator with delusions of godhood," the bearded man droned on, "but he's not soft!"

Unbelievable nerve—O'Brien felt a twitch of frustration run across his forehead.

The ensign at the Starfleet table tensed visibly, but the red-shirt stopped him from challenging the antagonizing man.

The waitress, looking overworked and nervous, came to them and asked, "What'll it be, boys? And don't say raktajino—if I have to say we don't carry that one more time—"

"Who ordered raktajino?" Odo asked vigilantly.

"The Klingons."

"Klingons?"

"Yes."

O'Brien looked around, as did Odo and Bashir, but he didn't see any Klingons. He glanced at Worf, who was noticeably twitching, but Worf said nothing.

"Right over there," the waitress said with an are-you-blind inflection.

She nodded to the table with the silverbacks sitting around it. A little surly, maybe, but Klingons? These men were no bigger than any average muscular human, and none had the Klingon turtle-shelled brow-ridge O'Brien had seen all his life. They had ordinary black hair. The uniforms weren't Klingon either, so far as he recognized. The only trait these had in common with Klingons was that every last one of them was bearded.

Bashir looked at Worf. *"Those* are *Klingons?"*

"All right," the waitress said gruffly, "you four have had enough. I'm cutting you off."

She turned on a heel and strode away spicily.

"Well, Mr. Worf?" Odo prodded.

Worf looked at him, then at Bashir, then O'Brien.

"They *are* Klingons," he admitted finally.

All three others looked again at the silverbacks, then they all looked again at Worf.

Klingons! That changed everything! Perhaps some disease had caused their personalities to migrate to the outsides of their bodies, because that man with the beard was prickling O'Brien like a cactus.

Worf fidgeted—and that was a sight. "It is a long story."

"What happened?" O'Brien pushed. "Some kind of genetic engineering?"

"Viral mutation?" Bashir suggested.

Twitching like an old lady now, Worf growled, "We do *not* discuss it with outsiders!"

O'Brien was about to spear him with another remark, but across the bar came the sharp scrape of a chair being shoved back. As he turned, he saw the younger officer in gold on his feet and glaring at one of the Klingons as if ready to peel the beard off hair by hair.

But the engineer at the table had the younger man by the arm. "Take it easy, lad. Everybody's entitled to an opinion."

Scottish. No doubt about that. Inverness, maybe. Someplace northish. Senior officer, too. No doubt about that either.

"That's right," the Klingon taunted, speaking very slowly, partly because he was drunk and partly because he was enjoying the surgery. "And if I think that Kirk is a Denebian slime devil . . . well, that's my opinion too."

O'Brien had seen this Klingon stalking the Starfleeters, but the order had been sent around the ship that there would be no trouble, and the Starfleet people in these bars were trying not to react to the picking and prancing of this one Klingon.

"Don't do it, mister, and that's an order," the Scotsman said firmly, holding back the young ensign who wanted to pull the Klingon's beard off.

"Look at the way Kirk is ignoring that Klingon," O'Brien mentioned admiringly. "He's letting the security officer handle it."

"Chief," Bashir murmured, "are you sure that's Kirk?"

"Absolutely."

"Then why is he wearing lieutenant's stripes?" The doctor held up his own sleeve and noted that the slashes matched the slashes on that other man's sleeve.

O'Brien peered across the room—and damn if Julian wasn't right. A lieutenant, not a captain! He was completely wasting a good slug of admiration!

"Of course," the Klingon was saying now, "Captain Kirk deserves his ship! We like the *Enterprise,* we—" He laughed. "We really do!" He confirmed with glances to the other men in silver tunics, then turned his invective to the man in red. "That sagging old rustbucket—"

Something inside Miles O'Brien clicked to full alert as fury boiled up from the pit. Insulting a man's ship!

"—is designed like a garbage scow! Half the quadrant knows it! That's why they're all learning to speak Klingonese!"

"Mr. Scott!" the ensign spat.

Now the man in red—an engineer! O'Brien's thoughts seized on what he was seeing.

"Montgomery Scott!" he choked. "My God . . . Montgomery Scott—it's Montgomery Scott!"

"Who?" Odo asked.

The Klingon raised his voice. "And if I think that the *Enterprise* is designed like a garbage scow, then that's my opinion, too."

Cautiously, Odo broke in with "I think we have bigger problems than a case of mistaken identity."

Across the room, the Scottish officer was involved in a slow burn. The situation was escalating, control blowing to the wind.

Yep, those were Klingons, all right. Delighting in torture no matter what their skulls looked like.

The Scot half-turned. There was a dangerous dare on his face.

"Laddie . . . don't you think you should . . . rephrase that?"

Tilting slightly forward, O'Brien got his feet under him and braced his legs. Strange, getting mad at something that happened a hundred-odd years ago. Oh, but wonderful, punching a few of those words back down a Klingon throat . . .

And there was the Klingon, who obviously knew perfectly well just who he was insulting. Fury built brick by brick until O'Brien was seeing only red. Criticizing an engineer's own personal work—his own ship! There was a line being crossed here, by damn!

The Klingon leaned teasingly on the bar, playing to his own crewmates as much as to the starship's chief engineer, speaking very slowly on purpose. "You're right. I should. I didn't mean to say that the *Enterprise* should be hauling garbage. I mean to say it should be hauled away *as* garbage!"

Enjoying his chance to pinch the fine hairs of a Starfleet officer, the Klingon reeled back in laughter, knowing he was free to prowl this station and that Starfleet personnel were not allowed to cause trouble based only on words.

But, oh, this was torture for O'Brien, this pretending not to be affected.

Then again, he was wearing an *Enterprise* crew shirt! He didn't *have* to pretend not to care!

Watching without a blink, he dug his fingernails into his palms. *Please, oh, please . . .*

The famous Scotsman slowly stood up.

Yes, yes—

The Klingon was still laughing, too drunk to notice that Montgomery Scott was on his feet.

When he turned, the Klingon wasn't on his feet anymore—in fact, his feet were on the table behind him, and the rest of his body was hanging over the other side.

The man O'Brien had mistaken for Kirk now burst to his feet and shoved two chairs out of his way, squaring off with the Klingons, who also came to their feet. Chairs scratched all over the bar.

As if propelled by some sorcerous force—for which he would've paid highly right now—O'Brien's chair flew out from behind him with Irish polite gentility, making easy room for him to dance. Worf jolted up as well, hands clenched, arms flexed.

"Gentlemen!" Odo warned. "What are you doing?"

O'Brien didn't even look at him. There wasn't time to explain either the choreography or the attraction of a good old-fashioned pub brawl.

Now that the truce was blown, Montgomery Scott made no bones about the fact that he'd committed himself. He picked another Klingon and roundly backhanded him into the carpet.

The bar broke into full-blown chaos, throwing the punches O'Brien so much wanted to throw himself. The young ensign climbed a table and launched himself at another Klingon, and it was on. The Scotsman was grappling the Klingon who had taunted them into this, and—

"Incoming!" O'Brien shoved Odo aside as another Klingon plunged at them. Cramming Odo under his elbow, he managed to take the body blow himself. Ah—a reason!

O'Brien staggered back, his battered chest aching, and took another punch that drove him back farther, but he rounded with a coiled fist and let fly into the Klingon's broad nose. God, that felt good!

As the Klingon dropped before him, O'Brien saw the bartender dodge past, heading out of the room, and a flash of Worf crashing about with two Klingons. That bartender would be going for help. There was only a minute or two—

O'Brien braced his back against the edge of a table

and pushed off, filling his hands with the silver tunic of the Klingon he was fighting. At first he hesitated, knowing Odo was still there and might be crushed if this Klingon were shoved backward—no, there was Odo, shimmying to one side, shaking his head. Good.

With a mighty heave, O'Brien growled, "Denebian slime devil!" and hurled the Klingon backward into the fighting mob.

The big merchant at the bar was dodging the fight and now found his way behind the bar, where he procured a couple of drinks for himself on the house. O'Brien noticed him particularly because there was a target Klingon exactly halfway between him and the merchant. Good as any.

Grinding out, "Tin-plated dictator, eh?" O'Brien lunged at the Klingon and landed the heel of his hand on the Klingon's chin, but the Klingon had seen him coming and braced himself for the blow. He spun, but didn't go down, then lunged for O'Brien. O'Brien was sucked off his feet and onto the defensive.

Fists flew and bodies spun all around him, and he took a hard blow to the back, then whirled.

"Garbage scow!" he snarled, and landed a fist into his opponent's left eye. The Klingon stumbled back and disappeared behind two other grappling forms.

O'Brien's arms ached, but a good ache. Been a long time. Just before he had a chance to enjoy the sensation, Julian Bashir flew past him and staggered against a particularly large Klingon who resented the attention. The Klingon grasped Bashir by both arms and spun him like a toy, then twisted the doctor's elbow into a vicious angle behind his back. Bashir's features crumpled in pain until a desperate gasp was choked out.

Enraged by what he saw, O'Brien gouged the heel of his hand into the eye of the Klingon who grappled him, spat, "Regulan bloodworm, right?" and lashed out with a foot into the kidneys of the Klingon twisting Bashir into a pretzel. The Klingon jolted, and Bashir spiraled sideways, then the Klingon turned on O'Brien.

As he joined the Klingon in a fierce dance, O'Brien tried to keep track of Worf and Odo, too—Worf would hold his own against these Klingons, and probably so could Odo, with all his experience in law enforcement on *Deep Space Nine,* but Bashir wasn't the physical type and would be quickly puréed. Rather than let the angry Klingon round on the doctor again, O'Brien launched onto the Klingon's back and straddled him like a cowboy bucking a bull.

We should get out of here while we can, he thought, but his fists were tingling for more and he couldn't make himself stop. *Only a few more seconds—*

An elbow caught him in the side of the head and knocked the precaution from his brain. The bar whirled crazily and he lost equilibrium, but knotted his fingers into the nearest Klingon's hair and held on for life and breath. In an attempt to shake him, the Klingon made a wild dash for the bulkhead, spinning at the last second so that O'Brien took the blow of the unmoving wall square in the spine.

As every nerve ending in his body blistered with

pain, he went numb all over and slid to the deck, tingling. Beside him, the door rushed open and several security guards came in running. The bartender followed them, and on his way in took one of the glasses away from the big merchant who was about to make use of the moment.

A few feet away, Odo suddenly grabbed Worf, pointed out the open door, and shouted, "It's Darvin!"

O'Brien shoved himself up on an arm and cranked around just in time to see the old man they'd been searching for dash out of sight. Amazing he could move that fast—

Shoving to his feet, O'Brien aimed for the door, but never made it. A Klingon tackled him, but this time he had his balance and pitched the Klingon off. He rounded on his opponent to drive home the point.

Instead he came face-to-face with one of the meaty *Enterprise* security officers. Fresh and ready, the security man had him in an instant bodylock. O'Brien's arms and legs still tingled, his breath coming in heaves, and he was caught.

Gathering himself for one more hard push, he entertained the notion of tossing off this one last man, then dodging for the door and clearing out before anything worse happened. If he could only get Bashir—

The guard's grip communicated very well that O'Brien could no more break away than fly away.

As he twisted to gauge distance, he made a plan to

break free and corral the doctor out of here, but the plan died aborning when he noticed Bashir already pressed to the wall by the forearm of another security guard. The fight was over. The trouble was just starting.

Busted.

CHAPTER
9

"BAR . . . FIGHT . . . TIMELINE . . . arrested . . . consequences—"

"Easy there. It's going to be all right."

"How can you say that, Dulmur? For all we know, we could be in an alternate timeline right now!"

Sisko watched the two time guys as near-panic surged and faded, then surged again. Their imaginations were going crazy, and he was enjoying the spectacle. Lucsly was lying on the office couch, pale and weak. Sisko brought him a cup of tea.

"Your men could've avoided that fight, Captain," Dulmur said.

From memory, Lucsly droned, "Regulation one-fifty-seven, section three, paragraph eighteen: Starfleet officers shall take all necessary precautions to minimize any participation in historical events."

"All right," Sisko allowed. "It was a mistake. But there were no lasting repercussions."

"How do you know that?" Dulmur challenged. "For all we know, we could be living in an alternate timeline right now!"

"If my people caused any changes in the timeline, we would've been the first to notice when we got back."

Wasn't that right? That was the way it had always been described to him—that people who went through a timeline change were somehow protected from the alterations. At least, that was the going theory.

"Why do they all have to say that?" Lucsly agonized.

Dulmur turned to Sisko. "So . . . your men were arrested?"

"I want to know who started it."

The voice cut through the middle of Miles O'Brien's spine, did a double somersault, and vaulted up to the back of his neck. How he could possibly have mistaken Lieutenant Freeman for Captain James Kirk, he had no idea. Especially now, as he stood in a lineup in the captain's office, with James Kirk pacing before them like a drill sergeant.

All faces were forward, all eyes focused flat on the bulkhead. No one dared meet the captain's eyes.

But O'Brien keenly felt the captain's eyes. There was no ducking the blinding glare of reputation.

James Kirk had neither imposing stature nor a Grecian musculature, yet he was compact and tightly strung. He looked strong and quick, and he strode the line of his errant crew like a bully on the street. In contrast to the way his legend had rumbled through history, the reality of James Kirk was a shock. He was no Viking, yet there was voltage in his presence, and this room was charged.

"I'm waiting," Kirk said, as he reversed his pace and came back.

No one said anything. Fate brought the captain to the center of the line, where O'Brien stood stiff as a graveyard cross, with Bashir at his side, both overstaring.

James Kirk's fierce eyes fixed on O'Brien's. "Who started the fight?"

With every fiber of his existence, O'Brien wished he were back in Father Fitzpatrick's parish, facing Sister Mary Asumpta. This was a dream. A mistake. A trick. Halloween. O'Brien was glad he was standing next to a doctor because he wanted very much to have a heart attack.

"I don't know, sir" was all he could think to say.

Never in his life had he been stared at by a man who knew he was lying in quite the degree that James Kirk knew. The captain moved on, but the eyes stayed for an extra second or two.

"All right." The captain went to the next man in the

line. The ensign, now with a bruise on his face. "Chekov. I know you. You started it, didn't you?"

"No, sir, I didn't," the young man said truthfully.

"Well, who did?" The words shot like pellets out of a weapon.

Ensign Chekov twitched, then smiled. "I don't know, sir!"

"I don't know, sir," Kirk muttered back mockingly.

They knew, and he knew they knew, and they knew he knew they knew.

"I want to know who threw the first punch," the captain demanded.

He reached the end of the twitching line, turned again, and walked slowly back.

"All right. You're all confined to quarters until I find out who started it. Dismissed."

The line of crewmen turned on a proper heel and marched for the door. As they filed into the corridor, O'Brien felt he was breaking out of prison. Would he remember how to breathe?

"Scotty, not you," the captain's voice broke, and O'Brien almost turned back automatically.

The door gushed closed and the crewmen dissipated without a word.

Bashir pulled him aside. "That was close!"

"Me!" O'Brien heaved, awestruck that he had been singled out and had spoken, in person, to James Kirk! "Out of all the people in the lineup, he asked *me* who threw the punch!"

With a sorry glower, Bashir deliberately tortured, "And you lied to him."

"I lied to Captain Kirk!" O'Brien agreed happily. "I wish Keiko had been there to see it!"

"Scotty, not you."

Engineer Scott drew up short at the captain's words. Trouble.

It was command-officer-to-command-officer time.

Jim Kirk saw the shame and resignation in his chief engineer's face as Scott hungrily watched the others leave and the door close, then turned reluctantly back to his captain. He'd almost made it.

Kirk squared off before him. "You were supposed to *prevent* trouble, Mr. Scott."

Miserably, Scott sighed. "Aye, Captain . . ."

Shifting to a more sympathetic mode—and no more nonsense—Kirk asked, "Who threw the first punch, Scotty?"

Dressing down Montgomery Scott wasn't easy. He had more years' experience than Kirk and could pull the ship apart and put it back together in a week and a half, and he took over command when Kirk and Spock were gone. That was a lot of trust to be scolding.

Scott inhaled, held it, then held it some more. "Umm . . ."

Surprised at the hesitation, Kirk quietly urged, "Scotty . . ."

His eyes working with shame, again Scott paused, resisting the question, but there was no getting around an answer. "I did, Captain," he said pathetically.

"*You* did, Mr. Scott?"

The engineer's eyes flickered with candid embar-rassment.

"What caused it, Scotty?" Kirk pressed.

"They insulted us, sir!"

"Must've been some insult—"

"Aye, it was!"

"You threw the first punch . . ." Kirk pressed his lips and shook his head sadly in mock astonishment.

Scott clarified, "Chekov wanted to, but I held him back."

"You held—why did Chekov want to start a fight?"

"Umm . . . the Klingons, they . . . is this off the record, sir?"

"No, this is not off the record!"

"Well, Captain, eh . . . the Klingons called you a . . . a tin-plated dictator with delusions of god-hood."

"Is that all?"

Suddenly anxious to prove that he'd had cause, Scott said, "No, sir, they also compared you with a Denebian slime devil!"

"I see."

"And then they said that you were—"

"I *get* the picture, Scotty," Kirk cut off sharply. He worked—hard—at keeping his face stern, avoiding showing the sniggering pride that his crew would brawl with Klingons rather than have their captain insulted.

Realizing he'd gotten carried away, Scott drew a breath and held it again. "Yes, sir."

Kirk battled with his facial muscles. Don't grin,

don't grin. "And after they said all this, that's when you hit the Klingons."

"No, sir."

Was that the careless drone of some damned bagpipe in the background?

Kirk frowned. "No?"

Like an errant boy with a slingshot behind his back, Scott said, "No, I didn't . . . you told us to avoid trouble."

"Oh, yes—"

"And I didn't see that it was worth fighting about. After all, we're big enough to take a few insults . . . aren't we?"

"What was it they said that started the fight?"

"They called the *Enterprise* a garbage scow!" the engineer offered, sneering at the taste of the words in his mouth. At the last moment, he added, "Sir!"

Beginning to realize just where he stood, Kirk accepted the sorry attempt to explain. "And that's when you hit the Klingons."

Relieved that the story was out, Scott sighed heavily. "Yes, sir!"

"You hit the Klingons because they insulted the *Enterprise,* not because they—"

"Well, sir," Scott said, fishing for understanding, "this was a matter o' pride!"

Pride . . . loyalty . . . oh, well.

"All right, Scotty. Dismissed. Oh—Scotty, you're . . ." He shrugged, because they both knew what and why. Kirk shrugged in some kind of mutual acceptance. "You're confined to quarters until further notice."

"Yes, sir," Scott said with obvious relief. They both knew this was only for the sake of the crew, just a token that would prove no one could break an order and receive absolution, but also to show that the brotherhood of officers did not stand together against the crew. A divided ship was no good to anyone.

Scott started to turn away, then broke out in a flashing smile. "Thank you, sir! It'll give me a chance to catch up on my technical journals!"

Damn. The point was just being missed here.

The engineer spun in delight and rounded for the door.

"Scotty—" Kirk called at the last instant.

"Sir?"

"Who were those two crewmen standing next to Chekov? The ensign and the lieutenant? Did they beam down with you?"

"Oh, must've, sir. I sent every detail down with orders—eh, well, I went down in the last bunch from this watch. I think those two went before me."

Strange. "Do you know their names?"

"No, sir. The one's, I think, a doctor, and the other must be in security, because he's not on my staff. We've had some visitors on board lately, sir, Dr. McCoy tells me."

"Mmm . . . too bad that they come on board and get involved in a fight first thing. Not the best report to show up on a man's record."

Scott took a step or two back toward him. "Well, sir . . . I'm the one who started the trouble. I'd be willing to take the blame. No need to name the men. They were pretty much sticking up for me, after all."

"Mmm." Kirk sighed.

"And it always takes me a few weeks to put names to faces. I'm sure it's the same for you, sir. Perfectly understandable."

"Yes, well. You'd better go, Scotty. Before I become any less understanding."

"Doctor, hello."

"Oh, good afternoon, Doctor. I thought you went down to the station."

"Yes, yes, I did, sir. But there was a . . . disturbance. Shore leave has been canceled."

Julian Bashir tried to look much more at ease in the sickbay than he actually felt. Ordinarily sickbays, hospitals, infirmaries, and clinics were second home. First home, more like. He'd skimmed trouble more luckily than O'Brien, but now they had to come up with an excuse to beam back down to the station and keep hunting for that Klingon. They knew he wasn't on the ship.

If they beamed out on their own, the ship's sensors would detect it. They had to get clearance. O'Brien dared not show his face after the episode with the Klingons and the captain. He'd already gained far too much attention, and that man they'd thought was a security officer had turned out to be Chief Engineer

Montgomery Scott, a man whose reputation in his field equaled James Kirk's in his. They'd brushed fate too closely, on two fronts.

Of course, Bashir knew the identity of this easygoing surgeon. Leonard McCoy of the *Enterprise* had broken many barriers in the medical field, logging thousands of hours of discovery, research, and conclusions about alien metabolisms, viruses, and other new revelations in medicine during the days when the *Enterprise* was venturing where no man had gone before.

All these men and women had reputations. The senior officers of this ship were famous. Other crewmen who had served any length of time aboard the *Enterprise* had been known to write books, go on lecture tours, become educators and explorers. As they grew older and became fewer and fewer, they were more in demand. Bashir himself had attended a lecture on deep-space medicine by a former intern aboard the *Enterprise* during James Kirk's third year as captain. That man had been very old at that lecture.

Today, that man's boss, Leonard McCoy, was in his forties and rosy with good health. His brown hair was thick and his hands strong, his forearms well defined by the short sleeves of the medical smock. He wasn't yet the legend of medical science who had tackled a thousand new things. In fact, at the moment, he was plucking at one of the little furballs.

And there were plenty of tribbles to choose from.

There were dozens upon dozens littering the sickbay now, clustered masses of puff balls from white to brown to pink, all purring and trilling in happy chorus with the throbbing of the ship around them.

"Still doing your biotechnics?" McCoy asked, without looking up from taking a sample of blood from a tribble.

"Yes, sir," Bashir lied. "I'll get back to it, if I'm not disturbing you."

"You're not. Funny . . ." McCoy was distracted by something in his readouts, and he was not very interested in Bashir.

That was good. Best not push.

He retreated to the anteroom with the computer terminal he had been working on before, knowing that this time it would do him no good. He had to pretend to work, then come up with a reason for McCoy to give him clearance to beam back to the station. Not clearance of such import that it would require reporting to the bridge, but enough clearance to override the canceled shore-leave order. And he had to have a reason for an assistant to come along with him, for O'Brien would have to come along. The transporter officer would have to receive clearance for two beamings from the chief surgeon.

Bashir sat down to think, and to appear to be working. Barely had the seat cushion compressed beneath him before the door panel opened in the outer office. He stayed quiet, and listened.

"Anything to report, Doctor?" came a deep voice.

"If I had anything to report, Mr. Spock, I would've reported it. At the moment, the only thing I have to tell the captain that's different from an hour ago is that now I have eighty-two tribbles instead of eleven."

Bashir peeked out into the other room very carefully, then suddenly became even more careful. That was a Vulcan. A Vulcan could hear him moving about in here, even moving softly.

He stood very still and simply listened.

"Yes," Spock said pointlessly. "My computations on them are becoming oppressively high. I have them here for you."

There was a pause, the hum and bleep of medical equipment, and a few moments of silence from the two science specialists.

Then McCoy asked, "What's the matter, Spock?"

Spock's voice was deep, unenchanted. "There's something disquieting about these creatures."

"Oh? Don't tell me you've had a feeling?"

"Don't be insulting, Doctor. They remind me of the lilies of the field . . . they toil not, neither do they spin. But they seem to eat a great deal. I see no practical use for them."

"Does everything have to have a practical use for you?" the doctor asked with disapproval. "They're nice, they're soft, and they make a pleasant sound."

"So would an ermine violin, Doctor, but I see no advantage in having one."

Pressed against the inner doorframe of the anteroom, Bashir smiled at the sparring.

"It is a human characteristic to love little animals," McCoy told him fiercely, raising his voice, "especially if they're attractive in some way."

"Doctor, I am well aware of human characteristics, I am frequently inundated by them, but I have trained myself to put up with practically anything."

Fielding the insult, McCoy straightened a little. "Spock, I don't know much about these little tribbles yet, but there is one thing that I have discovered."

"What is that, Doctor?"

"I *like* them. Better than I like you."

Without a beat, Spock parried, "Doctor, they do indeed have one redeeming characteristic."

"What's that?"

"They do not talk too much. If you'll excuse me, sir."

Outside, the door panel gushed open, then closed.

Amazing! They had been teasing each other! A Vulcan—teasing!

Fascinated by the exchange, Bashir almost went through the wall when his communicator chirped—at least Spock was gone. He ducked to the deepest corner and turned his face inward as he snatched for the communicator. Before the thing made any more noise, he flipped the grid open and brought it to his lips.

"Bashir," he whispered.

"Sisko here, Doctor. Odo caught Darvin."

"Where are you, sir?"

"Mess hall, Defiant."

"Can you beam me aboard?"

"Negative. Stay there. Keep a low profile. We may still need you aboard the ship. We'll contact you once we wring Darvin's plans out of him."

"Understood, sir. Happy wringing."

"Welcome back, Mr. Darvin."

Odo dropped off the *Defiant*'s transporter-bay platform and wrestled Arne Darvin, old or not, roughly down after him. On the other side of the old man, Worf had a grip on Darvin, too, and was even angrier than Odo. He crammed Darvin fiercely against the nearest bulkhead. Neither his nor Odo's mood improved any when they noticed that Darvin seemed completely happy and unconcerned.

"The pleasure's all mine," the disguised Klingon said.

Worf seemed ready to peel the disguise off, surgical or not, so Odo quietly warned, "Worf . . ."

Reluctantly, Worf turned the old man loose and took a cushioning step back.

Odo stepped into the empty space and faced Darvin. "You realize you're facing some very serious charges when we get back."

Darvin smiled. "You wouldn't dare put one of the greatest heroes of the Klingon Empire in the brig."

"You are no hero to the Empire," Worf thundered.

Looking up with the same smile, Darvin told him, "I will be. I've been thinking about my statue in the Hall of Warriors. I want it to capture my essence. Our statues can be so generic sometimes, don't you think?"

Feeling his own future melt before him, Odo said, "I take it, whatever your plan is, you've already set it in motion."

Darvin leaned back in the chair they'd pushed him into. "I see myself standing with Kirk's head in one hand, and a tribble in the other!"

Blistering, Worf leaned forward with unveiled threat. "What have you done? Did you hire someone to kill him? Did you sabotage the *Enterprise?*"

"Nothing so mundane," Darvin said. "I've had plenty of time to think about this, about what Kirk did to me and how he should die. Let me just say Kirk's death will have a certain poetic justice to it."

"Sisko here."

"Sir, we have him. His plan is already in the works."

"What's the plan, Odo? Did you get him to tell you?"

"Well, yes, Worf . . . squeezed it out of him. He intends to inflict poetic justice on James Kirk, by blowing him up with a tribble."

Sisko looked up at Dax. They were both pretending to work again, with the communicator perched inside an open drawer, out of sight of the crewmen crossing behind them. "He put a bomb in a tribble?"

"It's his 'revenge.' Originally, Kirk saw the way a tribble reacted to Darvin and realized he was a Klingon."

Odo sounded doubtful of hope.

"He wouldn't tell us where this tribble is," the

constable went on, *"but he did say it would go off within the hour."*

Glancing out into the corridor, Sisko was confronted with the same hopelessness. There were thousands of tribbles crowding the deck, and crewmen picked through them with dismay on their faces.

"It could be anywhere," he uttered.

"Benjamin," Dax said, "I think we should risk going to the bridge. If we can use the internal sensors, we could scan the entire ship for explosives in a matter of seconds."

Sisko nodded. Into the communicator he said, "Dax and I will take care of the *Enterprise*. The rest of you beam over to *K-Seven* and begin searching over there."

"Understood, but I think Mr. Worf should remain here. It seems that he's . . . allergic to tribbles."

"All right."

"Captain—" It was O'Brien's voice. He must be there, and that meant Bashir probably was, too. *"I don't think we'll be able to get to K-Seven's internal sensors."*

"Then you'll have to manually scan every tribble on the station."

"There must be thousands of them by now!"

"Hundreds of thousands." Yes, Bashir was there.

Dax nodded as if they could see her. "One million seven hundred and seventy-one thousand five hundred and sixty-one."

The voices on the communicator went silent. It was an audio stare.

Sisko gave her the visual one.

She bobbed her brows. "That's starting with one tribble having an average litter of ten every twelve hours. After three days, you'd—"

"Thank you," Sisko cut off. "You have your orders, people. Sisko out."

CHAPTER
10

THE PLAN WAS woefully inadequate. By the time Sisko found himself in the turbolift, standing with Dax and heading for the bridge, the muscles in his neck, arms, and back were all pounding from tension and a headache was beginning to percolate.

When the bridge doors opened, he drew a breath and had a hard time letting go of it. He was in shock. He almost forgot what he had come for.

He was stepping out onto the bridge.

The bridge of the *Enterprise*. Imagine walking out onto *this* bridge!

Its colors were simple, primary, tantalizing, and efficient, appointed in black here and there. The glossy black consoles were rimmed in a single line of red, and the lights and switches were clear and attractive. On the viewing trunks, the squarish monitors with their beautiful pictures of near-space, the bright red bridge rail in contrast to the blue-gray trunks and bulkheads, the soft lighting, and the bright colors of the crew members' uniforms all reached out and drew him into a mythical embrace. Across from where he stood, the big main screen was framed by its mounting, and an engineer strode across the picture, a brilliant representation of Deep Space Station K-Seven and the hovering Klingon cruiser beyond it.

This was the grandest ship—the first of her kind, the one which had taken the hardest knocks of early exploration. The actual first *Starship Enterprise.*

Sisko felt supremely and proudly human as he stood here. The sounds, soft whoops and blips of working machinery, each sound a subtle reassurance, all seemed familiar. He wanted to stand here and enjoy what he saw, smelled, heard, and what he felt. The sheer privilege of walking out onto this bridge . . .

A muffled trilling shook him out of his charm— there were tribbles everywhere, gently singing against the steady sounds of the starship's beautiful bridge. There were tribbles on the consoles, tribbles on the carpet, and tribbles crawling slowly along the bright red rail. Tribbles, tribbles, many colors, many sizes, all purring.

And one of them . . . or one of the other thousands . . .

Sisko sustained himself with his purpose and led

Dax to the forward port-side engineering console. She played the controls briefly, then quietly said, "You take the science subsystems station. I'll send you data for analysis and isolation."

"Where?" he asked.

"If I remember, it's over on the starboard side, by the main screen. Over there."

Trying to appear at home, Sisko crossed in front of the big main screen, avoiding the eyes of the navigator and helmsman, who at the moment didn't have much to do but maintain orbit about the station. No problem, except that the station had no notable gravity.

The navigator and helmsman paid him no attention. They were both groggily stroking tribbles.

Sisko took up post at the science subsystems monitor, noting with some trepidation the presence of Commander Spock off to his right at what must've been the main library computer console.

The Vulcan's presence was magnetic and held constant undercurrents as he sat quietly and worked his cooperative computer with legendary thoroughness. Sisko's hands were actually cold.

And colder still when the turbolift door whispered and James Kirk strode slowly onto the bridge. Lines of dissatisfaction grooved the captain's young face, as if he already sensed or even knew there was too much trouble brewing under these events.

For an instant, Sisko thought the captain was looking at him, but relief poured through as he realized Kirk was actually looking around at all the tribbles.

Kirk moved with enviable familiarity along the bridge rail and down to his command platform. Without looking at his chair, he dropped tiredly into it. There was a squawk of animal protest, and the captain instantly bounced back up and fished a tribble out of the command chair.

Sisko bit his lip, but nothing more happened. No explosion. Relief made Sisko smile. Well, relief and the whole spectacle of Jim Kirk sitting on a living squeak.

Kirk cradled the tribble, annoyance creasing his features, accepted a smile and shrug from Dax, then punched his comm panel. "Dr. McCoy, would you mind coming up to the bridge?"

He stood up then and prowled the helm, scanning the tribbles hypnotizing his helmsman and navigator.

Dax finished her work at engineering, picked up one of the old-style padds and crossed the forward bridge to Sisko.

"I rerouted the sensors," she said quietly.

"It worked," Sisko said, checking his instruments. "I'm scanning the bridge for the explosive. Nothing up here . . ."

Leaning forward, Dax plucked a tribble from his console. "That's a relief. When Kirk sat on that tribble, I half expected it to go off. They're so cute . . . I can't believe Darvin would put a bomb in one."

"Mmm," Sisko agreed noncommittally. "Nothing on the first six decks."

"Lieutenant Uhura," Kirk's voice cut through sharply, as he hustled with an armload of tribbles to the woman at communications, "how did all these tribbles get onto the bridge?"

Again Sisko witnessed a wonderfully human side to Kirk the legend, Kirk the commander. All this with the tribbles was, to Kirk, a bunch of nonsense. He was thoroughly human. He joked, he got annoyed, he got headaches, he had close friends, and occasionally he was just plain winging it. Like now. He had no idea what to do about an enemy that everybody wanted to hug and cuddle.

Sisko smiled. He liked this Kirk a lot better than the Olympian hero portrayed one hundred years later.

"I don't know, sir," Lieutenant Uhura was saying with a sheepish smile. "They do seem to be all over the ship . . ."

The lift doors opened and a medical officer came toward Kirk.

"Dr. McCoy!"

McCoy approached Kirk with an easy stride. "Yes . . . did you want to see me, Jim?"

Dax watched the doctor and squinted. "I know him . . ."

"Must be McCoy," Sisko said uselessly. "The ship's doctor."

She kept looking. "McCoy . . . McCoy . . ."

Kirk confronted his chief surgeon with two fists full of tribbles in the face.

"Well, don't look at me," McCoy protested. "It's the tribbles who're breeding. And if we don't get them off the ship, we're gonna be hip-deep in them."

Squinting, Kirk ordered, "Could you explain that?"

"Well, the nearest thing I can figure out is that they're born pregnant." He grinned. "Which seems to be quite a time-saver!"

Wearily Kirk murmured, "Well, I know, but *really . . .*"

"And from my observations, it seems they're bisexual, reproducing at will. And, brother, have they got a lot of will."

Sisko grinned again, and turned to hide it. The doctor was completely unintimidated by Kirk. So Kirk had McCoy, and Sisko had Dax. Maybe fate made sure that men on the cutting edge of adventure always had somebody to keep them from getting too filled up with themselves.

"Leonard McCoy—" Dax gulped suddenly. "I met him when he was a student at Ol' Miss!"

Sisko kept his voice down. "Who met him? Curzon?"

"No, my host at the time was Emony. I was on Earth judging a gymnastics competition—"

"Captain, I'm forced to agree with the doctor." Spock swiveled around, his arms folded and his posture surprisingly relaxed. "I've been running computations on their rate of reproduction and the figures are taking an alarming direction. They're consuming our supplies, and returning nothing."

"Oh, but they do give us something, Mr. Spock," Lieutenant Uhura protested. "They give us love!"

As the men glared at her in varying degrees of scoff, she added, "Well, Cyrano Jones says that a tribble is the only love that money *can* buy."

"Too much of anything, Lieutenant," Kirk said painfully, "even love, isn't necessarily a good thing!"

He shoveled his tribbles into her arms.

Uhura struggled not to drop her load. "Yes, Captain . . ."

"I guess he took my advice," Dax murmured, and smiled as Sisko looked up at her. "About becoming a doctor. I told him he had the hands of a surgeon."

"I get the picture." Now that he had armament for future teases, Sisko clicked off his console. "I've scanned every deck. The bomb's not on board the ship."

Dax straightened, and he saw the same worry in her eyes that he felt in his own. "It must be somewhere on *K-Seven.*"

Yes, he thought. Somewhere.

CHAPTER
11

"STOP THE LIFT."

Sisko waited until Dax grasped the controls and caused the turbolift cab to stop between decks. They'd gotten off the bridge only minutes after Kirk himself, Spock, and McCoy had also left. Staying on the bridge was too touchy.

He pulled out his communicator, which luckily was rigged with twenty-fourth-century scramblers and directionals. "Sisko to Odo."

"Odo here."

"Are you on the station?"

"Yes . . . unfortunately."

"Explain that."

"Sir, there is barely any visible floor left. The tribbles

are covering everything. Including the bartender. Is Captain Kirk all right so far, sir?"

"He was a few minutes ago, but of course that doesn't mean anything. He might have headed over to the station. If you see him there, contact me. The bomb's not on board the *Enterprise,* so it must be over there."

"We've only been able to get through two decks. We're running out of time."

Hearing the frustration and hopelessness in Odo's voice, Sisko glanced at Dax. "I can send more teams from the *Defiant."*

"It's not a question of manpower, Captain," Odo told him. *"It's a question of multiplication. The tribbles are breeding so quickly, we can't keep up with them."*

"Benjamin," Dax interrupted, "maybe we can narrow things down a little. Presumably, Darvin put the bomb somewhere he knows Kirk is going to be in the next half hour. If we stick close to Kirk—"

"He might lead us right to it."

"It's worth a try," Odo agreed, *"but there's no reason for us to stop searching over here."*

"Keep at it for now, Constable." Sisko closed the communicator and clasped the lift control. "Deck Five."

"It should be easy," Dax said. "All we have to do is follow Kirk and try to anticipate a little."

"Easy," Sisko said, "except that we don't know exactly where he is right now."

"He went to Mr. Lurry's office, didn't he?"

"That's what he said, but by the time we have Kira beam us over there, he could be back here."

"Or he could be right next to the bomb right now, and if we beam over, we could be killed, too."

"Old man," Sisko said, sighing roughly, "have I ever told you that your logic is a pain in the backside?"

"Daily, in one way or another."

"Yes, well . . . I'll contact Odo and have them check Lurry's office. If the captain's still there, they can track him. You and I will stay here in case he comes back."

He snapped his communicator open again, and realized that his hand was shaking.

"Captain Kirk, I'm mystified at your tone of voice! I've done nothing to warrant such severe treatment!"

"Oh, really?"

Jim Kirk wheeled around, noting a ring of desperation and a crack of fear in the voice of merchant Cyrano Jones.

Jones was a charming con man, an everybody's uncle, a licensed prospector, and a general haberdasher, and Kirk had an easy time rattling him by merely pacing in front of him.

In contrast to Kirk's tense pacing, Spock stood apocalyptically still with his hands behind his back. "Surely you must've realized what would've happened if you removed the tribbles from their predator-filled environment to an environment where their natural multiplicative proclivities would have no restraining factors."

Frantic, Jones gave Spock a pathetic, whole-body chuckle. "Well, of cour—what did you say?"

Spock blinked, glanced at Kirk, and tried again. "By removing the tribbles from their natural habitat, you have, so to speak, removed the cork from the bottle and allowed the genie to escape."

"If by that you mean do they breed quickly, well, of course, that's how I maintain my stock. But breeding animals isn't against regulations—only breeding dangerous ones. And tribbles aren't dangerous . . ." The big gentle man held up a tribble and cooed like a carnival caller appealing to children, desperate to make himself innocent in what had developed into a colossal pain in the neck.

"Just incredibly prolific," Kirk complained, having to grudgingly accept that there was some sense in what Jones said. He hadn't broken any regulations.

"Precisely!" Jones chimed. "And at six credits a head—that is, a *body*—it mounts up. Now, if you'll excuse me . . ." He got up and rounded for the door.

"You should sell an instruction and maintenance manual with this thing," Kirk muttered, as Jones handed him the tribble.

Realizing he was off the hook, Cyrano Jones's voice changed tenor. "If I did, what would happen to man's search for knowledge?" He punctuated the moment with a clap against one of his pockets, and said, "Well, I must be tending my ship. *Au revoir.*"

He swashed out of the room, crossing paths at the door with Nils Barris and Arne Darvin, who cast the prospector a cutting glare, then hurried into the room.

Darvin gave Barris an encouraging shove. "Go ahead, sir, tell him!"

"Captain Kirk," Barris began, shored up, "I consider your security measures a disgrace. In my opinion, you have taken this entire very important project far too lightly!"

Kirk bobbed his eyebrows and actually started to enjoy himself. "On the contrary, sir, I . . . I think of this project as very important. It is you I take lightly."

Fuming now, Barris leveled a finger at him. "I am going to report fully to the proper authorities that you have given free access to this station to a man who is quite probably a Klingon spy!"

His attitude shifted as Kirk said, "Now, that's a very serious charge. To whom are you referring?"

"To that man who just walked out of here."

"Cyrano Jones? A Klingon agent?"

"Did you hear me?"

"I heard you."

In the spirit of the moment, Spock supplied, "He simply could not believe his ears."

Kirk looked at him quizzically, and they exchanged a moment of mutual entertainment before he turned back to Barris. "What evidence do you have against Mr. Jones?"

Barris motioned toward Darvin. "My assistant here has kept Mr. Jones under close surveillance for quite some time and his actions have been most suspicious. I believe he was involved in that little altercation between your men and the—"

"Yes, yes, go on. What else do you have?"

"Well, Captain," Darvin began, "I checked his ship's log and it seems he was in the Klingon sphere of influence less than four months ago."

"The man is an independent scout, Captain," Barris persisted. "It's quite possible that he is also a Klingon spy."

Kirk handed the subject to Spock with a glance, and the first officer took over.

"We have already checked on the background of Mr. Cyrano Jones," Spock said with studious efficiency. "He is a licensed asteroid locator and prospector. He's never broken the law, at least not severely, and for the past seven years with his one-man spaceship he has obtained a marginal living by engaging in the buying and selling of rare merchandise, including, unfortunately, tribbles."

Barris would've pounded a table if he'd been standing near one. "But he is after my grain!"

"Do you have any proof of that?" Kirk shot back.

Darvin insisted, "You can't deny he's disrupted this station!"

"People have disrupted stations before without being Klingon agents. Sometimes all they need is a title, Mr. Barris. Unfortunately, disrupting a station is not an offense. Now if you'll excuse me . . ." Kirk handed the tribble to Spock, and gave a clap on an imaginary waistcoat. "I have a ship to tend to. *Au revoir.*"

"Are you sure he was headed in this direction?"

Sisko sat nervously at the rec-room table and looked around at the other *Enterprise* crew enjoying their off-watch hours by plucking, stroking, and cuddling tribbles.

Tribbles, tribbles, everywhere . . . on the deck, on the tables, on the processors, and even dotting the walls. He had no idea how they were crawling up the walls. He hadn't yet been able to find anything resembling a foot or tentacle or suction cup.

Dax sat across from him, tensely watching the door. "Odo tracked them to the station's transporter room. I tracked them out of the ship's. They came out of the transporter room and came down this corridor. I deduced they were coming right here. They could've stopped off at the sickbay, I suppose . . ."

"The man's life is in our hands," Sisko said, worried. "The life of one of the most famous men in Starfleet history. He has things yet to do that had better get done, or our universe is going to turn upside down the hard way. We've got to do better than this. If Darvin's estimation of an hour was right, we have less than ten minutes. And we can't even scan any of these tribbles without giving ourselves away."

"What do you intend to do, then? If we find Captain Kirk, and trail him to the tribble with the bomb, what can we do without attracting attention?"

"I'll attract it if I have to," Sisko told her, "to save his life."

She narrowed her eyes. "How are you going to explain that?"

Miserably, he sighed. "Feign insanity, I suppose."

What feign? Here they were, one hundred years in the past, trying to find an adorable fuzzy bomb before it killed one of the greatest adventurers in history and put an end to the universe as they knew it. Reality couldn't be this weird. Obviously, Sisko was strapped to a bed in some asylum, having paranoid delusions.

Feeling each second tick by a pulse at a time, his whole body tightened as the door panel opened and Kirk and Spock strode in together.

Suddenly lightheaded with relief, Sisko glanced at Dax, then watched the captain go to the wall replicators. "I'm so glad to see him," he murmured. "He's all right, so far."

"And Darvin's on the station, the young Darvin I mean, so how would he have known where the captain would be at this moment?" Dax murmured back. "It's got to be somewhere else."

"Shh . . ."

"My chicken sandwich and coffee . . ."

Kirk was holding a food plate loaded not with food, but with tribbles. He raised his coffee cup, with a little brown tribble stuffed into it.

He swung around to Spock. "This is my chicken sandwich and coffee!"

The Vulcan gazed down at his own plateful of tribbles. "Fascinating . . ."

"I want these things off the ship—I don't care if it takes every man we've got, I want them off the ship!"

Before Spock could respond, the door opened again and Engineer Scott shuffled in, with an armload of tribbles from his hips to his neck. "Aye, they're into the machinery, all right," he said. "And they're probably in all the other food processors, too."

"How?" Kirk asked.

"Probably through one of the air vents."

"Captain," Spock said urgently, "there are vents of that type on the space station."

A light came on in Kirk's face. "And in the storage compartments!"

At the table, Sisko hissed, "Storage compartments!"

He pushed to his feet, skirting the wall and leading Dax to the door as Captain Kirk ditched his tribbles and went immediately to a comm unit on a table.

As Sisko hurried out, he heard the captain's urgent orders filter away behind him.

"This is Kirk. Contact Manager Lurry and Nils Barris. Have them meet us near the storage compartments. We're beaming down. Come on, Spock!"

CHAPTER 12

THEY BEAMED DOWN to the station via *Defiant*'s transporter, then climbed down an access ladder through a dusty conduit, and the whole time Sisko felt as if he had to sneeze.

He didn't dare.

The deck gave under his boots as he lowered himself into the darkened storage vault, and he flinched as he realized he was stepping on a carpet of tribbles. Gently he lowered himself into a sea of fur and looked around, waiting for his eyes to adjust.

There was absolutely no grain left in the entire compartment. He couldn't speak for the other storage areas, but this one had been completely cleaned out by tribbles.

At least they were neat.

Without a word, he and Dax began scanning with their tricorders.

Sisko picked up a tribble, gave it a gentle squeeze. "Most of these tribbles," he observed, "are dead!"

The impact made him cold. Had the old Darvin done something? Were the tribbles supposed to be dead, or did Sisko have more timeline contamination on his hands?

They looked at each other. Had the tribbles suffocated? Crushed each other with their own weight? No, that didn't add up. Had they been electrocuted? Chewed into open circuits? Why would they be dead? Sisko glanced at his tricorder and found the answer: "The grain's been poisoned."

Dax checked her own tricorder. "I'm picking up a faint tricobalt signature," she said quietly. "I can't lock in on the signal, but the bomb's somewhere under here."

"Guard, is that door secure?"

Voices from outside, the deck below . . .

"Yes, sir. Nothing could get in."

"Good. Open it up."

Chirp.

Sisko looked up. "What's that?"

Lowering her voice urgently, Dax said, "Someone's trying to open one of the bay doors!"

The two backed up against a wall to avoid being seen once the hopper doors opened. This bay was built on angles, with doors at the bottoms of the sides, so anything inside would spill out automatically, like the old railroad hopper cars that carried grain. He and Dax edged away from those doors barely in time.

Should he try to hold the doors closed? If all these tribbles cascaded onto Jim Kirk and then one blew up, Jim Kirk's last moment was going to be a very undignified one.

The chirping noise came again, then again, and the doors slid laterally open beneath the mound of tribbles.

Like soup going down a drain, the tribbles siphoned downward, cascading out into the open corridor below.

Holding his breath and waiting for the big boom, Sisko dared a peek through the center of the drain and saw the top of James Kirk's head as tribbles by the hundreds poured upon him.

"Benjamin!" Dax motioned to the tribbles still waiting to fall. "It's right here—within a meter of where I'm standing!"

She started checking tribbles. Sisko scooted over to help, and to scoop tribbles away from the open hatch in hopes of keeping the critical deadly one from falling on Kirk.

Below, as the trainload of tribbles exhausted itself onto Captain Kirk, the captain's head and one shoulder emerged from a gloriously silly ten-foot-wide mound of furballs. Now just a few tribbles tumbled, one or two at a time.

What if the bomb had fallen? Sisko looked at Dax, but she was still testing tribbles remaining in the vault—the bomb must still be up here, or her readings would've changed.

He kept glancing down below, to keep aware of the situation, just as James Kirk turned his dismayed face upward.

He grabbed a small white tribble, scanned it and tossed it down. It hit Kirk on the top of the head and kept him from looking up.

Below, Commander Spock's voice filtered through the muted trilling of the few remaining live tribbles. "They appear to be gorged."

"Gorged?" Nils Barris was standing nearby, panic in his voice. "On my grain!"

Dax threw a large brown tribble out the door after testing it. *Bounce*—it enjoyed a perfect encounter with Jim Kirk.

"Kirk, I am going to hold you responsible! There must be thousands of them . . ."

"Hundreds of thousands," Kirk complained.

Spock evenly informed, "One million seven hundred seventy-one thousand five hundred sixty-one."

Sisko looked at Dax—a moment of congratulation as they hunted the trouble tribble.

Below, Spock explained, "That's assuming one tribble multiplying with an average litter of ten, producing a new generation every twelve hours for a period of three days."

Sisko dropped another tribble down the hole. It landed on Kirk's shoulder with a squeak, but the captain didn't look up this time.

"And that's assuming they got here three days ago," Kirk contributed, as Dax tossed another tribble down upon him.

"And allowing for the amount of grain consumed and the volume of the storage compartment."

"Kirk, you should've known!" Barris raged, as Dax pitched a big pink tribble out the hatch for a perfect four-pointer on Kirk's noggin. "You are responsible for turning the development project into a total disaster!"

"Mr. Barris—"

"And I am through being intimidated, Kirk! Now, you have insulted me, you've ignored me, you've—you've walked all over me!" Barris bubbled with fury as Sisko tested a little white tribble, found it bombless, and pitched it out. "You've abused your authority and you have rejected my requests! And this—*this* is the result!"

Kirk glanced at the white tribble and began. "Now, I—"

"I am going to hold you responsible for—"

"Mr. Barris, I'll hold you in irons if you don't *shut up.*"

"Jim!" Dr. McCoy came into the corridor as Sisko peeked down. McCoy was smiling. "I think I've got it! All we have to do is quit feeding them! We quit feeding them, they stop breeding!"

Silence briefly filled the corridor, with the exception of a squawk from a medium-sized blue-gray tribble as Sisko pitched it overboard.

Mournfully Kirk uttered, "Now he tells me . . ."

"Captain," Spock began, "this tribble is dead. And so are these."

"A lot of 'em are dead," McCoy noted. "A lot of them are alive, but they won't be for long."

"The logical assumption is there's something in the grain."

"Yes," Kirk said with a touch of purpose. "Bones, I want the tribbles, the grain, everything analyzed. I want to know what killed these tribbles."

"I haven't figured out what keeps them alive yet!"

Sisko dared to look down, accidentally pushing a white tribble down onto the captain. It squawked as it bounced off his shoulder.

Kirk didn't look up. He was strafing McCoy with a glare.

"All right." The doctor sighed. "If I find out anything, I'll let you know."

Dax tricordered a big brown tribble and ditched it out the door.

Suddenly Sisko blinked at his tricorder and at the tribble in his own hand. Was he seeing right in the dimness? Yes!

"Found it!" He pulled out his communicator. "Sisko to *Defiant.*"

"It's dead," Dax said, fingering the bomb tribble.

"Go ahead, sir," Kira's voice came over the communicator.

"We found the bomb," Sisko whispered urgently. "Lock on to my tricorder's signal and beam it into space!"

"Acknowledged."

Instantly the tribble and the tricorder both buzzed with transporter energy. To hide the sound, Dax pitched more tribbles down onto Captain Kirk. The tribble and tricorder disappeared, and Sisko held his breath, half expecting to hear and feel the detonation—but it would happen as far out in space as Kira could send it.

"That isn't going to do you any good, Kirk!" Barris said, gleefully furious. "This project is ruined! And Starfleet is going to hear about it! And when they do, they will have a board of inquiry and they will roast you alive!"

"Yes, well—" Kirk was cut off as Sisko pitched a tribble out.

"And I am going to be there, Kirk! To enjoy every minute of it!"

"Kira to Sisko. It worked!"

Sisko almost collapsed with relief and tried to start thinking again. They didn't dare to beam out themselves. That would take too much energy and make too much noise. They'd have to wait. In order to keep attention from turning up to them, he rolled the last few tribbles out the door to bounce off Jim Kirk.

"Yes, until that board of inquiry, I'm still the captain," Kirk proclaimed forcedly. "And as captain, I want two things done. First, find Cyrano Jones. And second—"

Sisko tossed one more tribble.

Raising a beseeching hand, Kirk begged, "Close that door . . ."

CHAPTER

13

"REALLY, CAPTAIN KIRK, I must protest this treatment!"

Jim Kirk looked around as two security guards hustled a protesting Cyrano Jones, cradling several tribbles, into Manager Lurry's office. "Ah, Mr. Jones, with an armful. A few questions—"

As the security guards put Jones in a chair, another voice burst through the opening door.

"Captain Kirk!"

Ah, Koloth. And his first officer, too.

Swinging to face them, Kirk snapped, "What do you want?"

The Klingon seemed to think he had something on him. "An official apology addressed to the Klingon High Command. I expect you to assume full responsibility for the persecution of Klingon nationals in this quadrant."

Kirk eyed him, unflapped. "An apology?"

"Yes. You've harassed my men. You've treated them like criminals. You've been most uncourteous, Captain Kirk. If you wish to avoid a diplomatic incident—"

"No, Kirk!" Barris pushed in from where he had been standing nearby. "You can't let him! That'll give them the wedge they need to claim Sherman's Planet!"

Spock, his voice like a balm on the abrasions of the moment, pointed out, "I believe that more than the word of an aggrieved Klingon commander would be necessary for that, Mr. Barris."

Kirk glanced over his shoulder at him gratefully.

"Mr. Spock," Koloth said, "as far as Sherman's Planet is concerned, Captain Kirk has already given it to us."

"Well, we'll see about that," Kirk told him. "But before I take any official action, I'd like to know just what happened." Attention turned to Cyrano Jones as Kirk stepped toward him. "Who put the tribbles in the quadrotriticale? And what was in the grain that killed them?"

"Captain Kirk, before you go on, may I make a request?"

"Yes?"

He pointed at the tribbles in Cyrano Jones's arms. "Can you get those *things* out of here?"

Not so much to ask. McCoy had reported that the

tribbles seemed to have a particularly jarring effect on Klingons, cutting to the core of their nervous systems with what sounded like pleasant trilling to everyone else.

Kirk motioned to the security guards, who plucked up the trilling balls and headed for the door. As the door opened, the guards had to step aside for Arne Darvin.

The stiff young assistant behaved as if startled that someone was crossing his path at a common door, then bodily flinched again as the tribbles in the guards' hands suddenly quivered and screamed.

The guards held back, and Darvin tried to step past them, but the tribbles shrieked fitfully.

"Remarkable—" Spock intoned.

"Hold on a minute!" Kirk ordered. He turned to Jones. "I thought you said tribbles liked everybody."

"They do!" Jones protested in a surprisingly honest tone. "The last time I saw one act this way was in the bar."

"What was in the bar?"

"Klingons! Him, for one," Jones said, pointing at Koloth's first officer, the man Kirk knew had been the chief antagonist in the bar fight.

Kirk went to the doorway and took two tribbles from the nearest guard. Darvin stood there unmoving, his arms tightly folded. Kirk strode back into the room, deliberately moving too close to Koloth's first officer. Sure enough, the tribbles rattled and screamed in his hands.

"Why, you're right, Mr. Jones," Kirk observed with undisguised glee. "They don't like Klingons!"

The door opened and Dr. McCoy came in, which enhanced Kirk's idea. He walked to Spock, and the tribbles purred happily. "But they do like Vulcans."

"Obviously tribbles are very perceptive creatures, Captain," Spock offered, playing along with style.

"Obviously." He turned and extended his experiment to Barris. "Mr. Barris, they like *you* . . . well, there's no accounting for taste."

Like a cat who'd just caught the neighborhood rat, Kirk turned to Darvin and the tribbles rewarded him with a piercing squeal.

"They don't like you, Mr. Darvin. I wonder why? Bones?"

McCoy brought his medical tricorder to Darvin and turned it on. "Heartbeat is all wrong . . . his body temperature is—Jim, this man is a Klingon!"

"Klingon?" Barris gasped.

Swelling with joy, Kirk leveled a victorious gaze on him. "I wonder what Starfleet Command will have to say about that. What about the grain, Bones?"

McCoy turned to him. "Oh, yes . . . it was poisoned."

Absorbing one more shock, Barris breathed, "Poisoned . . ."

"Yes, it's been impregnated with a virus. The virus turns into an inert material in the bloodstream. The more the organism eats, the more inert matter is built up. So, after two or three days it would reach a point where they couldn't take in enough nourishment to survive."

"They starved to death," Kirk concluded. "In a storage compartment full of grain, they starved to death."

"That is essentially it," McCoy said, rocking on a heel.

Prowling, Kirk fixed eyes with Darvin. Slowly he prowled the disguised young Klingon. "Darvin, you talk?"

The clean-cut spy attempted, "I have nothing to say."

Kirk shoved the tribbles into his face. They sirened and waggled until Darvin winced.

"All right! I poisoned the grain! Take them away."

"And the tribbles had nothing to do with it."

"I don't know. I never saw one before in my life. And I hope I never see one of those fuzzy miserable things again."

"I'm certain that can be arranged, Darvin," Barris said indignantly. "Guards!"

The two security men sprang to life, now with a real criminal to guard, and shuffled Darvin out of the room.

Barris offered Kirk an almost polite farewell. "If you'll excuse me, Captain."

He followed the guards out, his attention on a new target of his antagonism now.

"Captain Koloth," Kirk began, "about that apology . . ."

"Yes?"

"You have six hours to get your ship out of Federation territory."

Anger flared across Koloth's face, but Kirk pushed the tribbles an inch closer, enough to set them off.

As physical pain and emotional infuriation streaked across Koloth's face, the Klingon offered a bare salute and hurried out of the room, with his first officer virtually running after.

As Spock, Jones, and McCoy surrounded him, Kirk felt the annoyances of the past few hours pour off him just as the tribbles had poured out of the storage bin.

"Y'know," he said happily, "I think I could learn to like tribbles!"

CHAPTER
14

"AFTER THE BOMB was detonated, history resumed its course."

As Ben Sisko wrapped up his story, he delightedly noted that the time cops had aged a couple of years in about an hour. Lucsly looked ill and Dulmur just looked older.

"Captain Kirk confronted Darvin," he continued, "and uncovered the fact that he was a spy. Captain Koloth took his ship back to the Empire with his tail between his legs, and by the time we returned to the *Defiant*, Major Kira had discovered how to use the Orb to bring us back to our own time. She found the key in one of the passages from the Prophecy of Kandal—"

"And that's when you returned to the present?" Dulmur asked, hoping, exhausted.

Sisko paused, studied their two faces and tried to measure whether or not they could take one more shock. He got a sudden vision of the two of them each in their own quarters in the dull offices of the Time Investigations Bureau, waking up in cold sweats for the next month.

Oh, what the hell.

"Well," he said, "not exactly. Before we left, I realized there was one last thing I had to do. Something I'd been thinking about ever since I saw that ship on the viewscreen . . ."

The bridge was appealing, nostalgic. The proportion was just perfect. Captain's chair at the center; helm officers in front so the captain could give orders quietly to them, but they would never fail to hear him, science station at his right, communications behind him, engineering at his left; and other systems monitors flanking the brilliant panorama of space on the main screen directly before the command arena.

As he stood amid the simple beauty of the old bridge, Ben Sisko felt as if he had stepped into a truly new frontier, the days when even near-space was a furnace, when rules and regulations were far away and the captain had to be autonomous whether he liked it or not.

A thrill surged through him as he realized the tantalizing adventures that still lay before these people around him, and he fought down a thunderous desire to stay here with them, and go.

The thrill turned electrical as the lift panel opened and Captain James Kirk took command of his bridge, pausing briefly on the aft quarterdeck. Sisko realized as he stood at the forward monitors that he was looking at Captain Kirk, Mr. Spock, Dr. Leonard McCoy, and Engineer Scott standing together within a pace of each other.

"Captain," Spock greeted from the engineering station, and the captain paused. "Starfleet was able to divert that freighter."

"Good. That means Sherman's Planet will get its quadrotriticale only a few weeks late."

Spock followed him as Kirk dropped to his command platform and vectored into his chair—at the last second, he stopped, braced on the chair's arms, and looked at the seat. Nothing in the captain's seat but the captain's . . . seat.

And no musical pigeon coo anywhere.

He glanced about with a new eye. "I don't see any tribbles around here."

From the upper bridge beside Scott, Dr. McCoy happily told him, "And you won't find a tribble on this entire ship, Jim."

"Bones!" Kirk lauded joyously. "How did you do that?"

McCoy sauntered to the lower deck, arms folded passively. "Well, I cannot take credit for another man's work. Scotty did it."

"Scotty!" Kirk chimed. "Where are the tribbles?"

Scott paled a shade or two and shifted the responsibility again. "Oh . . . Captain, it was Mr. Spock's recommendation."

"Of course." Kirk looked around to his right. "Mr. Spock."

Spock parried, "Based on computer analysis, of course, taking into account the possibilities of——"

"Gentlemen," Kirk broke in, "I don't want to interrupt this mutual admiration society, but I'd like to know where the tribbles are."

"Tell him, Spock," McCoy urged.

Hesitating, Spock grew uncharacteristically stiff. "Well, it *was* Mr. Scott who performed the actual engineering."

"Mr. *Scott.*"

The engineer uneasily crossed to the steps and came down to the captain's left side as Kirk insisted, "Where . . . are . . . the tribbles?"

Scott's expression was pathetic. "I used the transporter, Captain."

"You used the transporter?"

"Aye."

"Well, where did you transport them?"

Getting the idea there was an answer no one wanted to tell him, Kirk's eyes flared as he looked from Scott to McCoy, who suddenly gained an interest in the ceiling, then to Spock, then instantly back to the engineer, and he shifted in his chair. "Scott, you didn't transport them into space, did you?"

"Captain Kirk!" the engineer said hurtfully. "That'd be inhuman!"

"Well, where are they?"

"I gave them a very good home, sir."

"WHERE?"

"I gave them to the Klingons, sir."

Kirk's eyes widened, brows up. He gushed, "You gave them to the Klingons?"

"Yes, sir. Just before they went into warp, I beamed the whole kit and caboodle into their engine room. Where they'll be no tribble a'tall."

Every breath was held, every person wondering what the captain would say, what he would do, what he would conclude. Sisko found himself watching Engineer Scott, sure he'd seen that same expression on Miles O'Brien at least once.

Then Kirk crossed his legs, rested back, and smiled.

Behind them, Communications Officer Uhura let out a little sniff of laughter, which traveled virally to McCoy, then to Scott, still on the hot seat.

Kirk glanced at Spock, then cuffed Scott in the breadbasket and laughed, too.

Even Spock, standing at the captain's side with his arms emblematically folded, rocked from one foot to the other in sudden relaxation.

At the fore of the bridge, Sisko broke out in a smile as he hovered over his sensor hood, pretending to work. Kirk had a sense of humor! And so, apparently, did Mr. Spock. He made a mental note to add this poignant detail to the official historical logs. Posterity should know about something like that.

After a few elongated moments of mutual entertainment, Kirk said, "All right, we can consider ourselves absolved. Helm, make your course six-five mark two and adjust for arch. Let's sweep the Klingon border once before we move on."

"Aye, sir," Chekov said, still grinning.

Spock went to his station at the science console, Uhura went back to hers, Scott escaped all the way out to the turbolift, and McCoy went with him.

The captain sat grinning for several more minutes, and it took Sisko every one of those seconds to mount up the urge to go through with his daring though simple plan.

Shoring himself up with a deep breath, he picked up the nearest padd and a stylus, then turned and stepped down to the lower deck.

The instant Sisko encroached upon the command sphere, Kirk's sharp hazel eyes lanced to him. Struck with the import of that attention, Sisko almost backed up.

No, there would be no second chance.

"Excuse me, Captain," he said, dismayed that his voice sounded hoarse.

Kirk blinked. "Lieutenant . . . Lieutenant—"

"Benjamin Sisko, sir." He handed Kirk the stylus and padd, hoping the captain would just sign it without bothering to read it. "I've been on temporary assignment here," Sisko said tentatively. "Before I leave, I just wanted to say . . . it's been an honor to serve with you."

Kirk finished signing, then handed the padd back to Sisko and smiled. "All right, Lieutenant. Carry on."

Sisko wanted to say more, but at that moment Mr.

Spock turned and came to the rail as if about to address the captain, and that was just pushing too much. Without further dawdle or gawk, Sisko mounted the aft steps and marched into the waiting turbolift.

He quivered with satisfaction as the lift doors closed and he raised his communicator to signal the *Defiant,* and drew his last long sigh of *Enterprise* air.

Now he had the one prize he had always imagined to be out of reach—

Captain James T. Kirk's autograph.

"Captain."

"Mr. Spock."

"I thought you might like to know," Spock said as he came to the lower bridge, "Captain Koloth's ship has just crossed back into Klingon space and shows no sign of reducing speed or altering course."

"Mmm," Kirk acknowledged. "I wonder if he knew about Darvin."

"Possibly," Spock said. "His boldness at demanding shore leave on a Federation station was unprecedented. It's possible to theorize that his presence here was calculated, allowing him to take possession of Sherman's Planet once the poisoned grain was distributed. A Klingon presence in the sector would be difficult to play down. Dr. McCoy suspects the poison in the grain may be of the brand which would contaminate the soil, and not just the yield, thereby rendering the planet useless for at least a solar year, giving the Klingons ample time to establish claim."

"Well, I'm glad we stopped it," Kirk said casually. "It's somebody else's headache now. Nils Barris's, I hope. By the way, Spock—"

"Sir?"

"Who was that lieutenant who just left the bridge?"

"Pardon me?"

"That tall fellow who just left. What'd he say his name was? Brisko? Operations?"

"I'm not familiar with any Lieutenant Brisko in the operations division, sir."

"He said he was on temporary assignment."

Spock nodded. "We did do a recent exchange with the *Hood,* and Captain Dodge told me he was passing along some officers for additional training who had come to him from another starship. I cannot confirm at the moment that one of them was Brisko. I will do so, if you have concerns."

"No, no, don't bother," Kirk said, and paused. "It's just that . . . he didn't carry himself like a lieutenant."

Having no response to such subjectivity, Spock simply waited for the captain to come to a conclusion.

After a moment, Kirk dismissed the question and offered his first officer a canceling wave. "Not important, Spock. Don't let it trouble you."

CHAPTER

15

"Now, IF YOU want to put a letter of reprimand in my file for that," Sisko said, "go ahead."

Dulmur and Lucsly exchanged a look of helpless concern, communicating to each other and to Sisko that there really wasn't anything they could do about all this, even if Sisko had decided to stay in the past beyond the requirements of his mission.

They could confiscate his autograph, though, and thus he wasn't about to tell them he had it.

"We'll have to review the case," Lucsly said eventually, as if there were much else he could say, "before making any recommendations."

"However," Dulmur put in, "I don't think there was any harm done." When both Sisko and Lucsly looked at him, he admitted, "I probably would've done the same thing myself."

Dulmur blushed at his own ultimate transgression, but Lucsly didn't say anything.

Lucsly closed his briefcase in silent conclusion and stood up. The two time cops let Sisko lead them to the door without further comment on the terrible crime of having pushed the envelope of risk in time.

"There is one thing, Captain," Dulmur asked as the door opened before them.

"Yes?" Sisko encouraged.

Dulmur slowly began, "In regard to Captain Kirk . . . what color was his uniform?"

Sisko looked at them blankly for a moment, giving them an instant of terror that he hadn't paid any attention. Then he simply said, "Green."

The time guys looked at each other again, eyes wide with secret pleasure. Lucsly smiled and made a diagonal motion across his own chest—and, yes, Kirk's shirt had been the wraparound kind.

Dulmur swallowed a giggle.

"What does that have to do with the case?" Sisko tormented.

Instantly the two dropped their delight and tried to act serious.

"Nothing," Lucsly admitted.

"The important thing," Dulmur said, "is that your trip into the past had no lasting repercussions here in the present."

Uneasily, forcing himself not to grin, Sisko shifted

and led them out of the office, through Ops, toward the turbolift. In the background, Dax and Kira looked up expectantly, then controlled their curiosity.

"You'll be receiving our report in about a month," Dulmur said. "But based on what you've told us, I don't think you have anything to worry about."

"I'm glad to hear it," Sisko said.

"Goodbye, Captain."

"Goodbye."

The two guys stepped into the lift, and Lucsly said, "Docking Port Seven."

The lift closed and hummed, taking the investigators nice and away.

Dax and Kira were at Sisko's side before the sound faded. "It went well?" Dax asked.

Sisko only nodded.

"Good," Kira said. "The constable wants to see us on the Promenade."

Sisko looked at her and nodded. "I wouldn't be a bit surprised."

The Promenade. Quark's bar. Home Sweet Station.

Sisko led Kira and Dax out into the public area on the first level, and Odo was there to meet them, looking grim. The door to Quark's bar hung open, and the constable was gazing passively in, but didn't seem anxious to actually go in.

"Did you tell them?" he asked.

"They didn't ask," Sisko said. "I'm open to suggestions, people."

"We could build another station," Dax suggested.

Luckily, no one had the bad taste to suggest a really big barbecue.

Inside the bar, the Ferengi bartender Quark stood behind his bar, staring as if hit with phaser stun. His gnomish face was creased with unhappiness, and upon his misshapen head rested a cooing, purring tribble.

Not such a problem, given the shape of Quark's head, but for the tribbles on the bar—over a hundred at first glance—and the thousand more tribbles on the tables, on the floor, in the kiosks, on the chairs, in the pitchers and carafes, and dotting the very walls.

There were even more than this morning.

Sisko and his crew stood as if iron-bound, staring as the carpet of tribbles inched toward them and slowly swarmed around their feet, jockeying for a cuddle.

Sisko pressed a grin flat. He glanced to the upper-level walkway, where Lieutenant Worf glared down in disgust.

"Well," Sisko decided, "This is just part of the life on a deep-space station. One of the many trials and tribble-ations we face every day. Suddenly I feel like having a chicken sandwich and some coffee. Anyone care to join me?"

Afterword
by
Ronald D. Moore

Today I walked the corridor of the *Starship Enterprise* and sat on the bridge. Not the A,B,C,D, or E, mind you—the original. *Constitution* class. The finest ship in the fleet.

Down on Stage 11 is an exacting replica of the fabled vessel that started it all, and I must tell you the ghosts of *Star Trek* past were all around us. The background players are walking around in bright red, gold, and blue uniforms . . . there's a sign for Mr. Kyle's quarters . . . the triangular ladders hidden away in alcoves lead to other decks . . . wall coms are sprinkled along the way . . . turbolifts stand ready. To walk the Corridor is to at once step back and step forward in time. It's the future, the twenty-third century. And it's the past, the 1960s. Somewhere between memory and fantasy, the *Starship Enterprise* plies her five-year mission. It's their ship—Kirk, Spock, McCoy, Shatner, Nimoy, Kelly, Roddenberry, Justman, Coon, Jeffries, Feinberg, and all the others. It's our ship—Sisko, Picard, Janeway, Brooks, Stewart, Mulgrew, Berman, Piller, Behr, Taylor, Klink, Menosky, West, Oster, Cameron, Okuda, and many others. And it's your ship—Trimble, Winston, Gerrold, Nemecek, Altman, Whitfield, Caputo, Carey, Ford and everyone who's ever raced to make it home in time for another rerun or said "Kirk to Enterprise," with the faint wish that Scotty's voice would really answer. This one's for us. The fans. The people who love that beautiful lady almost as much as Kirk did.

And this one's for you, Gene. Thank you for thirty years of joy. And I hope we make you proud.

—Ronald D. Moore,
Fan